THE LONG HIGH NOON

BOOKS BY LOREN D. ESTLEMAN

Kill Zone
Roses Are Dead
Any Man's Death
Motor City Blue
Angel Eyes
The Midnight Man
The Glass Highway
Sugartown
Every Brilliant Eye
Lady Yesterday
Downriver
Silent Thunder
Sweet Women Lie
Never Street
The Witchfinder
The Hours of the Virgin
A Smile on the Face of the Tiger
*City of Widows**
*The High Rocks**
*Billy Gashade**
*Stamping Ground**
*Aces & Eights**
*Journey of the Dead**
*Jitterbug**
*Thunder City**
*The Rocky Mountain Moving Picture Association**
*The Master Executioner**
*Black Powder, White Smoke**
*White Desert**
Sinister Heights
*Something Borrowed, Something Black**
*Port Hazard**
*Poison Blonde**
*Retro**
*Little Black Dress**
*Nicotine Kiss**
*The Undertaker's Wife**
*The Adventures of Johnny Vermillion**
*American Detective**
*Gas City**
*Frames**
*The Branch and the Scaffold**
*Alone**
*The Book of Murdock**
*Roy & Lillie: A Love Story**
*The Left-Handed Dollar**
*Infernal Angels**
*Burning Midnight**
*Alive!**
*The Confessions of Al Capone**
*Don't Look for Me**
*Ragtime Cowboys**
*You Know Who Killed Me**

*A Forge Book

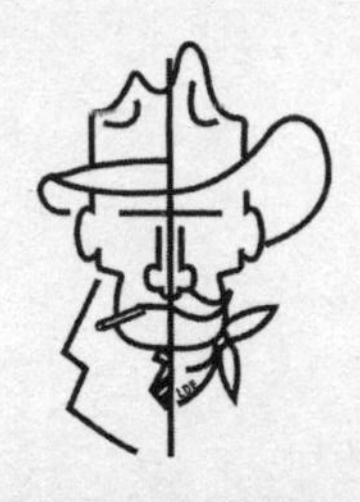

Loren D. Estleman

THE LONG HIGH NOON

A Tom Doherty Associates Book
New York

This is a work of fiction. All of the characters, organizations, and events portrayed in this novel are either products of the author's imagination or are used fictitiously.

THE LONG HIGH NOON

Designed by Mary Wirth

A Forge Book
Published by Tom Doherty Associates, LLC
175 Fifth Avenue
New York, NY 10010

www.tor-forge.com

The Library of Congress Cataloging-in-Publication Data
is available upon request.

ISBN 978-0-7653-3455-8 (hardcover)
ISBN 978-1-4668-1339-7 (e-book)

Forge books may be purchased for educational, business, or promotional use. For information on bulk purchases, please contact the Macmillan Corporate and Premium Sales Department at 1-800-221-7945, extension 5442, or write to specialmarkets@macmillan.com.

First Edition: May 2015

Printed in the United States of America

0 9 8 7 6 5 4 3 2 1

To the memory of Jory Sherman;
a force of nature, now
inexplicably stilled

Love is a kind of warfare.

—Ovid

THE LONG HIGH NOON

ONE

You never get a second chance to make a good first impression.

No one but Randy Locke and Frank Farmer knew just what it was that had blackened the blood between them, but it didn't lose its kick with time.

That it had to do with a woman suggested itself right away, and when fifteen years after their first run-in Abraham Cripplehorn christened her Mississippi Belle, the legend was complete. The fact that the writer/promoter had named her after the boat he kept in Gulfport was universally overlooked: Romance is everyone's weakness.

Money was the inevitable second suggestion; but ranch hands didn't covet it, only the fun that comes with it, and the effects didn't last long enough to justify violence.

If either remembered the actual cause, it rode drag behind the standing strategy, which was to annihilate the other man whenever the pair wandered onto the same plot of real property. It was the one fixed thing in a changing

West, and it was in place so long, and was so thoroughly a part of their alchemical makeup, I really think they got so they could smell each other across a slaughteryard.

Most likely whatever set them on the prod happened when both were working for the old Circle X in south Texas just after the end of the Rebellion, potting and being potted at by Don Alvarado's vaqueros across the border over cattle of indistinct claim. Randy and Frank were a close match with pistols, although Frank had the edge with a carbine after years of sniping Confederates from trees. He saw it as a point of honor not to use that advantage over Randy, because he didn't want suspicions of imparity to take the shine off dancing a jig on his enemy's grave.

Physically, the two were indistinguishable from the lot that flocked to the big ranches looking for work in those heady early years of the North American cattle trade. Randy was short and thick, and had the distracting habit of blinking constantly, his eyes being sensitive to sun and dust, which were the principal exports of the desert Southwest after stringy beef and chili peppers that burned like fire ants going down and like molten iron coming out. He favored Mexican sombreros with umbrella brims to cut some of the glare, and which some of his less-sensitive colleagues said made him resemble a roofing nail. Randy is generally reckoned to have been about twenty-two at the time of that first confrontation. Frank was lean, looked taller than he was because of his long legs, but when he sat a horse his hat came level with Randy's when he rode alongside. Both men sported whiskers, Randy's on the slovenly side, Frank's trimmed into neat imperials whenever a barber was handy. The entry of his birth in the family Bible in Pennsylvania put him at twenty-four in that year of 1868. He was tidy in his dress and grooming, whether he was wearing wool worsted or faded dungarees. His fellow hands said he could roll in cowflop on Saturday afternoon and take a duchess to a dance Saturday night. They called him Lord Percival when he was out of earshot: He was too good with a long gun, and his fists when it wasn't inside reach, to chance it otherwise. He told Shuck Ballard he spent half his wages on boots and tailoring.

"What about the other half?" Shuck asked.

"Frittered away on fool things."

Curiously, Randy, round-faced and not given overmuch to hygiene, seldom wanted for female company of his own. It wasn't unusual for him to enter a saloon with one on his arm, and sometimes both.

"I treat 'em like ladies, that's the secret," he said. "I always take off my socks. Sometimes they don't even charge."

When that got back to Frank, he curled his lip. "That little stump'd have to pay a sheep."

The first time they turned their pistols away from Mexicans and on each other was in the Bluebottle Saloon in El Paso, from either end of the fifty-foot bar the owner touted as the longest west of St. Louis. Both missed, being of an alcoholic temperament at the time, but stout Randy corrected that the next morning when he rousted lanky Frank out of a tub of bathwater in the Cathay Gardens on Mesa Street and broke one of his short ribs with a .44 slug when Frank lunged for his Colt in its holster hanging on the back of a chair.

He recovered, of course, or our story would end here, and he went looking for Randy, who'd been turned out of the outfit for shorthanding it just before the drive to Kansas, when every man jack was worth twice the price of his string. (The Circle X foreman, George Purdy, was infamous for solutions that doubled the original problems. He wound up a state senator in Indiana.) Frank caught up with Randy in a stiff Wyoming winter in the middle of wolfing season and shot his horse out from under him—a result of windage, which is easier to miscalculate when you're using a short gun at a distance. The horse rolled over on Randy, dumping fifty dollars in bounty pelts lashed behind the cantle and shattering his leg.

This a little more than evened the account, because while Frank's wound had healed, leaving him with nothing worse than a throbbing misery when it snowed or rained, Randy's injury left him with a limp and not much prospect of ranch employment unless he put in for cook, and prolonged exposure to greasy fumes gave him the Tucson Two-Step, and an unfortunate nickname among the hands. He reckoned that as one more charge against Frank's side of the ledger.

As it happened, though, Randy's fortunes improved as a direct result.

The buffalo harvest was coming to its summit, with the Industrial Revolution going full tilt back East and in perpetual need of leather to make the belts to drive the gears of its manufactories, lap robes selling like tortillas among the carriage trade, and the army offering to redeem empty cartridge shells for cash in order to offset hunting expenses and encourage the starvation of the pestiferous Indian. If the winter was long enough and the thermometer stuck on zero, the big shaggies grew coats that dragged the ground and made an enterprising man's fortune in a season.

Randy oiled his good Ballard rifle, bought an elmwood wagon and four months' worth of tinned sardines and peaches, and set off for the prairie with an experienced skinner and a half-breed guide. They prospered. Notwithstanding the inconvenience of a three-month head cold and one frostbitten cheek that never did heal completely, Randy's share when they sold their first load of hides came to more than he'd seen roping and branding semi-tame bovines the previous four years.

The breed guide, who for unexplained reasons went by the name of Prince Robert, asked him how he intended to invest his share.

"Now I know how to hunt buffler, I'm fixing to spend every last dime tracking down Frank Farmer, putting a slug in his brain pan, and curing his hide in the hottest sun I can find this side of Pharaoh—and the other side, too, comes to that."

Prince Robert didn't pursue the point. He'd spent months of nights hearing his charge muttering Frank's name in his sleep, modifying it in terms that would shame a Virginia City bullwhacker. In the language of his Pawnee father, the guide referred to him in his thoughts as Snake-Who-Drinks-His-Own-Venom. He got his fill of it after one season, turned down the offer of another at twice the percentage, and signed on with the Seventh Cavalry, with whom he spilled out his life's blood on the field the Sioux and Cheyenne called the Greasy Grass; no doubt thanking the Man Above with his last breath he didn't have to listen to Randy Locke consigning Frank Farmer to Hell Everlasting any more.

Needless to say, Randy's happier financial condition hadn't made him grateful to his nemesis. He knew that game leg was not the result of an altruistic act. If anything, prosperity gave him the luxury of turning his attention from the humdrum concern of survival to refining the details of his vengeance. Over open fires he chewed on buffalo tongue, pretending it was Frank's liver, and whenever he rode into a town to pick up supplies and provisions, he circulated a description of the man he hated among all the locals.

They weren't much help, being locals and not inclined to travel and gather news in those brief few years when railroad construction was progressing at a crawl against natural obstructions and hostile tribes determined to eject the white man from their ancestral hunting grounds. If anything, his zeal for information made some of them suspect him of being a bounty-killer, one of those flightless raptors the war had spewed out into the frontier, or worse, a lawman, and the rare drifter who might have been persuaded to part with a valuable morsel of intelligence took it on the scout because there was paper out on him offering a reward over some little misunderstanding in some other territory. The winter went by with no response to Randy's queries beyond blank faces and shrugs and the occasional fast exit aboard a lathered mount.

This made him poor company even among the women, who had reason enough to hate their own and sense enough to chalk it up to circumstances beyond their control. There followed a long dry spell between feminine comforts.

Frank meanwhile was working for the Kansas Pacific Railroad, grading track and keeping his Winchester handy to pick off Sioux raiding parties through that same buffalo country. It's quite possible that he and Randy spied each other at a distance without realizing it; since the great brutes had grown too wary of man to venture within a thousand yards of a rowdy construction gang, the man who hunted them altered his course wide upon spotting one at work.

True, there were times when these men paused in the midst of reloading or spitting out coffee grounds, turned their faces to the wind, listening—sniffing?—for something familiar and despised, then shook their heads and returned to the necessity of the moment; both were still too new to the sensation of blind hatred to trust their instincts completely. And so once again their reunion depended upon fate.

TWO

Should auld acquaintance be forgot?

At this point you may be wondering who I am.

It's my fault, for slipping into first-person a while back, violating every journalist's rule about not making yourself a part of the story; but try as I will I can't figure a way to strike out the reference.

Well, we know what's the oldest profession, but storytelling surely comes next. The guy had to tell *some*one, and he wasn't about to tell it as if it happened to someone else.

I'm a writer, or I've tried to be. I joined the Circle X a few months after Randy Locke and Frank Farmer pulled out, leaving behind their legend. I was just off two semesters with the Columbia School of Creative Writing, and eager to glean firsthand experience to fuel my work; but my superabundant vocabulary made me a suspicious character in the bunkhouse, and my time there ruined my grammar for anything but sensational fiction. My bedroom is papered with rejections from *Frank Leslie's Illustrated Newspaper* and *The New England Journal,* among a dozen others, and sometime or other it dawned on me that I wasn't the next Mark Twain. I labored with Buffalo Bill's Wild West, grinding out fanciful tales of William F. Cody's adventures under the house names of Prentiss Ingraham and Ned Buntline for the gift shop, and a generation later scenarios for Thomas Ince and—for six delirious days—D.W. Griffith.

In between I waited tables in railroad hotels, tended bar in Denver and Las Vegas, New Mexico, battled bedbugs the size of lobsters in the county jail in Nebraska City, and sweated out six months in a laundry in San Francisco—cheek-by-jowl with the great Jack London, although I didn't find that out until much later, when Jack was too famous for me to approach with a humble request for a reference—and in all that time I could count the number of times I actually laid eyes on Randy Locke and Frank Farmer on the toes of Long John Silver's foot. Well, that's more than anyone else you could name. I guess you could call me a pilot fish, sucking the saltwater sweat off a couple of sharks who are all but forgotten in the great current of history's ever-rolling ocean.

My name? Forget it. You would anyway, five minutes after I told it. But I can make one unique claim: I'm the only soul living who can tell you anything you want to know about the longest gunfight in the history of the American West.

Not that you'd want to hear it. Their names don't resound with the thunder of a Wild Bill Hickok or a Wyatt Earp or even a Neanderthal like Clay Allison, who had the good grace to end his murderous bullying ways under the wheels of his own wagon when he was too drunk to hold his seat at the reins. As a result, my name wouldn't ring any farther than a lead nickel bouncing across shifting sand.

But I was there, and where were you?

When the K.P.R. spur reached Abilene, Frank put in for provisions—not before stopping in the establishment of a German tailor to order a Prince Albert coat, three linen shirts, and two pairs of striped trousers—and was emerging from the mercantile with a double armload of bacon, coffee, and one hundred rounds of ammunition, when he heard a familiar voice.

"Farmer! Palm your piece!"

Randy was smoking a cigar he'd just purchased from the profit of his latest delivery of hides. It was smoldering in the corner of his mouth when he dropped his hand to leather. Frank let go of his packages, meat, beans, and ordnance spilling into the gutter, and went for his hardware. Both men drew simultaneously; their reports sounded as one.

Frank's slug grazed Randy's collarbone, missing the big artery on the side of his neck by a quarter inch, and exiting out the back, taking along a measure of flesh and muscle.

Randy's aim was higher still in his haste, and sliced off the top of Frank's left ear.

Both men required medical attention, but because Randy's condition was more serious he was still recovering on a cot in the room behind the doctor's office, a place of yellow oak, square bottles of laudanum and horse liniment on shelves, with a reek of alcohol as solid as any of the furnishings, when he opened his eyes to see what appeared to be a two-headed demon coming through the door with a pistol.

This doctor was a great proponent of preventing infection by enveloping fresh wounds in yards of gauze and white cotton; a toe severed in a wood-cutting accident was good for a rod, and the victim of a serious miscalculation by a barber had tottered out of the office looking like a giraffe with a cut throat. Another inch or two of wrap and Frank Farmer wouldn't have gotten his injured ear through the doorway.

Randy, fogged up as he was with tincture of opium, had sense enough to know that devil or mortal enemy, the intruder was cause for swift action. He rolled off the edge of the cot an instant before his pillow exploded. With the air filled with feathers, disinfectant, and the stink of spent powder, he managed to grasp the lip of his white-enamel chamber pot and skim it in the general direction of his assailant.

He was lucky in the trajectory. Frank yelped.

The cry woke the doctor, an addict to his own painkillers who had passed out in his horsehair leather desk chair from the effects of self-treatment. He lurched to his feet and after some groping found the door to the back room, then managed to manhandle Frank back into the office. This and the action of disarming him took place somewhat more easily than it might have under most circumstances, because the chamber pot had struck Frank's mangled ear as surely as if it had been aimed with precision rather than hurled in blind panic. The fiery pain distracted him, making him easier to manipulate.

A summons to the law in the persons of a marshal freshly retired from buffalo skinning and two deputies who'd served with the Army of the Potomac deposited Frank in jail. There inside bars made from flat steel strips held fast by rivets, the doctor opened his bag and amputated the rest of the ear with one snip of his scissors, the heavy projectile having nearly finished the job.

Frank, remember, was vain of his appearance. He kept his teeth clean with baking powder when he could get it, yellow soap when powder was unavailable, and took a bath every other week when he was in town. When the flesh healed, he borrowed the use of a catalogue belonging to the doctor and ordered a prosthesis from a medical supply firm in San Francisco. It arrived three weeks later, a shell-shaped object molded from pink gutta-percha in a small box with the firm's name stamped on it in gold with instructions for its care and application. These required fixing it in place with a daily dosage of sealing wax, which had a demoralizing habit of softening and letting go in the heat, usually at inopportune times. He fell to keeping it in his pocket when he wasn't in civilization or among strangers. The inconvenience and its humiliating nature put Randy's account deep in the red, to Frank's estimation.

"An eye for an ear," he told the man in the cell adjoining his.

"That ain't exactly what the Book says," replied the other, who was in for lascivious conduct in broad daylight with a Rumanian woman.

"Randy Locke ain't exactly in the Book."

But payment was delayed.

By the time Frank was released from jail, Randy had returned to the buffalo hunt, conscious of the fact that his shooting arm needed time to recover before he took on anyone more challenging than a dumb brute. He was off to Nebraska, with a new skinner who wasn't nearly as stimulating company as the old, but the other man had found work with another outfit while Randy was down. This time Randy didn't hire a guide, the plains all being pretty much alike, down to the yellow-ocher grass and the same clapboard saloon, livery, and mercantile everywhere there was water enough to breed mosquitoes. He carried neither maps nor a compass. A man who couldn't identify the North Star when he saw it might as well wear a stiff collar and live in town.

Frank's fine for disturbing the public peace emptied his poke, so he rode back to the railhead to shoot Indians and grade track. The first gandy dancer who kidded him about getting his ear bit off by a Texas Street whore got a slug in his foot for his joke; the foreman who bound the wound, a former medical orderly with the Fifth Mississippi Volunteers, told him he was fortunate that Frank was saving his homicidal impulses for Randy Locke. Their relationship, with some healthy encouragement from bored newspaper publishers, was by this time entering the country of frontier legend.

The buffalo meanwhile were entering the country of the extinct.

The bottom didn't fall out of the market so much as it fell out from under the buffalo. Where the great herds had darkened the plains only a few years before, spilling over the nearest rise like thunderclouds rolling down from the Divide, little now remained but scattered bones. Soon even they were gone, scoured by pickers to sell by the ton to manufacturers to pulverize and run sugar through to remove impurities and to press and bake into fine china. Few easterners realized they owed their sweet pies and Christmas table dressings to a tick-ridden beast. Overnight, it seemed, the stacks of stiff green hides vanished from pole barns put up by buyers, and the buyers themselves disappeared into other enterprises, usually on one or the other coast by way of the new Transcontinental Railroad.

Randy drank up half his profits in a succession of establishments given to that practice, gambled the other half away on games of chance, and took his meals and shelter serving time in various jails for drunk and disorderly. One early morning he woke up in an alley in Omaha with his boots missing, his pockets turned inside out, and a hangover the size of Texas.

"Never too late to make a fresh start," he said, fumbling for his watch and finding the silver chain snapped in half and the timepiece gone.

But the ranches he applied to all had cooks they were satisfied with, and the work he picked up loading grain-sacks into wagons and swamping vomit and sawdust off saloon floors staled after a week or so. For a time he panhandled for money for drinks, food, and lodging, in that order, but after a couple of months his clothes looked like livery rubdown rags held together by rotten thread, dirt crusted his face and hands, and he stank like spoiled potatoes. There were no women in his life to bail him out when he was pressed into a work gang for vagrancy, shoveling horseshit out of a stable in which the county sheriff had a half-interest and cutting the throats of steers for a butcher whose brother-in-law sat on the bench of the circuit court. It was a lot of sweat and time, and none of it brought him an inch closer to Frank Farmer and the end of their transactions. He reckoned at that point he'd hit stony bottom.

Frank wasn't finding life any easier.

After the buffalo ran out, the Indians returned to reservations to subsist on government rations, when they weren't being embezzled by unscrupulous traders and Indian agents from Washington. The raids on survey parties and track-layers fell off, and with it the demand for sharpshooters to defend against them, particularly with the army taking up the slack, rounding up strays from the reservations and providing the same protection on the taxpayers' ticket that Frank had supplied for wages. The Great Undertaking having been completed at Promontory Point, the railroads laid off men in hordes, including part-time graders like Frank.

When he was offered work by the Santa Fe line as a common guard, dozing in some stuffy strong-car hoping for an assault by a gang of highwaymen just to break up the monotony, he demanded the time he had coming and rode to the nearest poker game. In a mining camp in Colorado he shot and killed a man over one pat hand too many and barely escaped a lynch mob when the deputy who'd arrested him, a naïve New Hampshire native lured West by dime novels, changed clothes with him and took his place in the cell while Frank left by a back door. (The mob, which had come there to lynch *some*one, strung up the deputy.)

Frank got away on a wind-broken bay he'd managed to steal from a corral, without a firearm or a cartwheel dollar to his name, just the clothes on his back and his Saturday-night ear in his pocket. He camped out under the stars, avoiding towns where the Thunder Creek Committee of Public Vigilance might have shinplasters out on him offering a reward for his hide, and stoned jackrabbits to survive.

His skill with a piece of shale did not measure up to his

marksmanship with a carbine. In the wee hours of a frosty Colorado morning he started awake, convinced Randy Locke was standing over him aiming his Colt between his eyes, and in his panic kicked dust at a scrubby jack pine. When he recovered his senses he knew the vision for a hallucination caused by hunger, aided by a dose of Rocky Mountain Spotted Fever. Wasting away, his belt buckle scraping a gall in his spine, burning hot when his teeth weren't chattering, skin bleeding where he'd scratched it raw, didn't distress him so much as the prospect of squandering his last hours fighting ghosts instead of Randy.

He calculated he was as low as low got.

Then God opened a window.

THREE

**A houseguest should never arrive empty-handed,
nor should a host point out the fact.**

Two windows, actually.

Frank's sabbatical in the wilderness turned out to be a stroke of luck. A team of young prospectors found him close to death and brought him to their camp, where the old witch woman who ran the laundry nursed him back to strength with some remedies she'd learned in Albania. During his recuperation she told him, in broken English, of a drifter she'd treated for a fractured skull that had remained undiagnosed since he left Utah Territory weeks earlier. It seemed it had been laid open by a wolfer named Locke with a bottle in Salt Lake City over some difference of opinion the patient couldn't remember. The description he'd given her matched Randy.

The old woman let Frank repay his debt working the washboard, and when he was well enough to travel gave him a bear's-claw necklace she'd made as a hex against bad luck. From there, walking and accepting rides from passersby, he went to Pueblo, where he traded the necklace to a greenhorn for a toothless roan, which got him as far as Grand Junction before it keeled over and died. He stock-clerked in a general merchandise store for a month, bought a decent mount and a Remington revolver with a cracked grip but not too much play in the action, and lit a shuck for Mormon country.

While the buzzards were still sizing Frank up in Colorado, Randy Locke was fattening his bankroll in Wyoming. He had what happened to the buffalo to thank for it.

Its population swollen by the easy life of gorging on millions of skinned carcasses left to rot, the Great Plains Wolf crunched down the last overlooked bone and turned its attention to cattle. The ranchers objected, and offered hefty bounties for fresh pelts.

Randy, who was no stranger to wolfing, approved, and in the case of some white-muzzled veterans shrewd enough to avoid traps and poison, cashed them in for rewards worthy of a gang of human desperadoes. Soon he could afford to dine in the best restaurants in Laramie and Cheyenne and sleep between clean hotel sheets every night he wasn't working.

He could afford to, but he didn't.

The improvement in his finances didn't extend to the habits he'd acquired as a piteous drunk. Waiters served him only at back doors, where the stink of old guts on his rags wouldn't offend fellow diners, and hotel clerks refused him accommodation entirely. He slept in stables and out in the weather and practiced his draw for hours, wearing down the scar tissue that slowed his right arm. In his impatience he shifted back and forth until he could clear leather and hit his mark with either hand as well as most men did with the one they favored.

It wasn't the wolves he was practicing for. The local species was dying so fast it was getting so all a man had to do was give one of them a mean look and it would roll over and kick itself still. It had taken the white man a century to kill off the buffalo, but only two years to send the Great Plains Wolf to extinction.

Poisoning was the cause more than hunting. With meat herds falling prey to the packs, it was considered a breach of good manners to venture out on any sort of errand without including a bottle of strychnine crystals in one's gear. If a man came upon a carcass that still had meat on its bones, he tainted it. A single crystal killed more scavenging grays than an experienced hunter with a repeater.

People, too. A fellow down on his luck found out his fortunes hadn't changed when he fed his family a loin of windfall venison and watched them contort and die. The frontier was a hard place, harder still with the arrival of Man.

A great shift was taking place. The Indian problem was all but settled: President Grant had authorized the plan of General Terry, Captain Benteen, and Colonel Custer to bottle up the Sioux and Cheyenne nations in an obscure valley in Montana Territory, the wild beeves had been cleared to make room for domestic cattle, and predators were reduced to roving independent operators named Hardin, James, and Younger, with bounties on their heads like the wolves themselves. Homesteaders were fencing in the open range, building schools and churches on grounds formerly reserved for pagan worship. Soon the frontier would be as much a part of dead history as tricorne hats and powdered wigs. If a man stood still and pointed his ears toward the East, he could hear the earth turning.

But two men refused to stand still. When they had food in their bellies and full pokes on their hips, each had the other in his craw.

When Wyoming Territory ran scarce of lobos, Randy crossed into Utah, where he busted a jug of Old Pepper over a fellow's head for commenting on his odor and when the law came looking for him withdrew above the treeline to trap and shoot wolves. He gave his victim a month either to die or to get better and the tin stars to lose interest, then returned to the city on the big lake to sell his pelts, celebrate his prosperity, and ponder where to start looking for Frank Farmer.

Who was looking for him.

The Latter-Day Saints were close-mouthed in the presence of strangers, particularly when they were asking about other strangers: The whole population seemed to deny any knowledge of English when Frank pleaded for help finding his long-lost brother, who couldn't be reached to be told of their mother's death, and kept its hands at its sides when he offered money.

Mormons weren't supposed to partake of hard liquor, but he found that not to be universal his first night in Salt Lake City when he lifted flat-brimmed hats off men sleeping in alleys, looking for a familiar round face with a squint. All he got was tangled beards, fermented breath, and best wishes on his salvation.

"Save the saving for yourself," he said, dropping their hats back onto their faces.

He was about to give it up as a cold trail when a druggist he bribed with a double eagle, a skinny gentile with ears like a ewer and an Adam's apple that stuck out like a third elbow, told him he sold two bottles of snakebite medicine nightly to a tramp who answered Randy's description.

"As a rule I'd offer him a snake just in case," said the pill salesman, "but he stinks up the alley. The cats are starting to complain."

"Where's he hang his hat?"

"Don't know and don't care, just as long as it's downwind."

The sun was sinking toward the flats, painting purple fingers on the brine.

"He been in yet tonight?"

"Never by daylight. He got into some kind of trouble a while back, but why he bothers to wait for dark I can't say. You can smell him before you see him."

"Wolfers stink and no mistake."

"Not like this one. He smells like his heart's corrupted clear to the center."

"That's my man."

"Why you'd want him is the question. I'd refuse him, even if the accounts wouldn't balance at the end of the week, but that blink of his gives me the fantods. He's crazier'n a foaming dog."

Frank flipped another double eagle—his last—and held it out. "I'll have two bottles and your apron."

"That all? You can have the skullbender for a half-dollar and my apron for free. I change 'em by the week, on account of the strychnine."

"That and a seat by the back door for an hour or two."

The druggist looked at the cracked butt of the Remington sticking out of Frank's belt. "I don't want no trouble."

"This buys plenty."

The jug-eared man worked his Adam's apple, then agreed to the bargain.

Frank smoked what was left of his tobacco sitting on a three-legged chair inside the door to the alley while the proprietor ground prescriptions and entered numbers into his big ledger up front. His boy came in from a delivery and he told him to go home.

"What about that case of codeine you wanted me to unpack?"

"I unpacked it. Things are slow."

"Well, I left my schoolbag in back."

"It'll keep. Tomorrow's Saturday."

When the druggist came back to make sure his visitor wasn't stuffing his pockets with tablets and tongue depressors, he saw the bottles were still unopened.

"Ain't you going to take even a swig?"

Frank shook his head. "You don't mess with your bait."

"It's getting late. Maybe he ain't coming."

"You said he came every night."

"I told you he's crazy."

"Who told you I ain't?"

"You can have your double eagle back, and you're welcome to the liquor. I'm commencing to think that coin's jinxed."

"Suit yourself, but I'm sticking." Frank stretched his arms above his head, bringing the butt of the Remington into view.

"My mama told me I'd catch my death in Utah. I was just too full of piss and vinegar to listen."

"A man should listen to his mother, then shut up about it when he didn't."

The jug-eared man returned to his accounts and prescriptions.

It had been full dark three-quarters of an hour, and the druggist kept hauling out his turnip watch and looking at it, then at the front door, which was two doors down from the marshal's office, when someone knocked on the alley side.

Frank got up so quickly the chair tipped and almost fell, but he caught it before it could make a noise that might spook his quarry and set it carefully back on its legs. He bent, picked up the bottles, and cradling them in his left arm, used that hand to turn the knob while with the other he drew the secondhand pistol from under his apron.

He put it away in haste.

A young woman stood in the alley wearing a red wrap over tarnished sequins and feathers in her hair. Her face was painted and she smelled as if she'd fallen into a rain barrel filled with lavender and toweled off with verbena leaves. It wasn't the rank odor Frank had expected, nor the form and features to go with it, and when she smiled at him, showing a gold tooth, and thrust out a handful of coins, he reached for them automatically; he was broke, after all.

The woman stepped to the side then, revealing the leering, filth-smeared visage of Randy Locke with its leprous patch of frostbitten cheek, crouched behind her stinking to high heaven and fisting his Colt. Fire flew from the muzzle.

FOUR

A gentleman never sees his name in a newspaper.

The impact of the shot slung Frank on his back. Miraculously, the bottles were spared, rolling harmlessly across the pinewood floor to a stop at the base of a crate filled with headache powders, where the druggist rescued them and placed them back in inventory, snakebite apparently being very common on the shore of the Great Salt Lake and the source of a large percentage of his income. It was a cinch the customer who'd paid for them wouldn't have any more use for spirits where he was headed.

The doctor, a respected elder in the Church of All Saints, a Godlike fellow with snowy hair and beard and eyes as blue as the lake, despaired several times of his patient's recovery, from the moment a pair of solid citizens carried him in, with a fly crawling undisturbed on his face, through several relapses just when it looked like he might be turning the bend. At the finish he thought about submitting a paper on the case to the *American Medical Journal* in Boston, but on reflection he reckoned it smacked of pride.

The slug lay close to the heart, too deep to reach through the chest, and had to be extracted through the back with a sure and steady hand. Dr. Elgar was sure of his hand, but not of the network of nerves that propelled the fingers; he eschewed strong drink, being a man of deep faith and conviction, but he'd reached his threescore and ten and the copper bracelet he wore on each wrist didn't appear to have made much headway against creeping rheumatism.

Many hours of surgery were required. Fatigue and self-doubt on top of his swollen joints led to tremors and many breaks for rest were necessary. Much blood was lost, and although some discoveries had been made in the science of transfusion, blood types remained a mystery. Many a rabbit and white rat had sacrificed itself to no progress at all.

When at great length the bullet was free with no damage to the heart or spine, infection set in, complicated by pneumonia. This doctor had served with the Prussian Army in Jena, and knew rather more about enteric fever, and not enough about its treatment, than he cared to admit. Frank's temperature soared. The sheets he lay on were as hot to the touch as boiled linen, and poultices were applied and removed with no sign of success. Telegrams went out to leaders in the medical field. One suggested leeches; another suggested the leader who'd suggested them should be burned at the stake as a reverse heretic. A Viennese physician who was turning his attention to the health of the mind wired in favor of cocaine, then sent another cable canceling the first. During this exchange, Frank's fever broke; but whether the poultices and soaking his sheets in ice water had anything to do with this reversal of fortunes no one could say.

"Ach!" pronounced the doctor. "Perhaps there is a God after all, and He is less judgmental than advertised."

During his long recuperation, in a makeshift hospital established in a back room of the ornate Mormon Temple, with a ponderous crucifix leaning out from the wall above his bed like the Sword of Damascus, the patient learned that Randy had caught wind of Frank's search, anticipated the trap he'd lain, and bought the services of a woman of dubious occupation to confuse him and slow his hand. Randy had ridden out of town directly his mission was accomplished, long before a citizens' commission could be appointed to pursue him.

In all likelihood, he thought his enemy was dead.

Upon regaining his strength, Frank worked off his obligation to the doctor by sweeping his office and scrubbing his medical instruments. It occurred to him that he'd spent most of his working hours paying out the expenses of his recovery from ailments related directly to Randy. This scarcely softened his opinion of the central fixation of his life.

By the time Frank's debt was dismissed, Randy's trail

might as well have led across an icepack. He struck out in search of employment and a place to bide his time until news surfaced of the whereabouts of his ancient antagonist.

Seasons passed before Randy discovered that he'd failed to lift the burden of Frank Farmer from the world.

In Carson City, Nevada, he celebrated his victory with a long, blistering soak in a bath house, got a shave and haircut, bought himself a complete new wardrobe and a valise to pack it in, and secured first-class passage in a Pullman coach to San Francisco, that sinkhole of pleasure. He'd saved enough by eating simple fare and staying out of hotels to keep his wolfing profits largely intact, and there was no better place to burn money than the Barbary Coast. He leaned back against the plush headrest and dreamt about good whiskey, friendly cards, and accommodating women. It was his first holiday since Appomattox.

Unnoticed by the pair in their relentless determination to destroy each other, the West had begun to extract a deep fascination from the East: The faster it barreled toward past history, the keener the curiosity among those in a position to monitor it from a safe distance.

Custer's spectacular finish, gun battles in the gold camps and cattle towns, and the expertly managed exploits of a saddle tramp who called himself Buffalo Bill, had kindled a blaze of interest that demanded fresh fuel by the week. It was only a question of time before a running gunfight that had involved the same two men for more than a decade aroused journalistic notice.

Randy had made the rounds of San Francisco's saloons, music halls, opium dens, and bordellos for weeks. It was like attaching a hose to his pockets and reversing the pressure, sucking out coins and paper currency with marvelous speed. His capital was so low it had to stand on tiptoe to peer over the gutter. He'd moved his baggage to a hotel far less lavish than he'd grown accustomed to, with roaches the size of cigar butts, rooms separated from their neighbors by two sheets of wallpaper, and a woman's false eyelash cemented to the basin in the dry-sink. He stretched his funds by rescuing yesterday's *Examiner* from a trash barrel and came upon the following paragraph in the local section:

> It has come to our editors' attention that Mr. Randolph Locke, the notorious Texas pistoleer, is visiting our city and at last word was stopping at the Eldorado Hotel. Readers familiar with our telegraph columns will recall that Mr. Locke and Mr. Frank Farmer, also originally of Texas, have been taking target practice upon each other across the map of the western states and territories since the spring of 1868. Mr. Farmer was last reported in Salt Lake City, U.T., taking the salt air and recovering from the most recent mortal attack upon his person by Mr. Locke.

The maid assigned to Randy's room—the widow of a forty-niner, Henrietta by name—complained to the hotel manager that she'd been forced to pick up hundreds of torn fragments of newspaper that had been flung about the premises before she could begin dusting.

The manager yanked a bale of hair from a nostril and examined it against the sunlight coming through the painted glass in the lobby door. "That's your job, if I recollect correctly."

"Sure, and I wouldn't mind it so much if I didn't hear the man that done it taking the Lord's name in vain all the way down the stairs."

Randy's chagrin upon learning that he'd failed to finish the job in the drugstore was exacerbated by the army of newspaper reporters who tracked him to his current lodgings, each crying for an exclusive interview. Wearing their trademark bowlers and ripe unwashed linen, they laid ambush for him in the lobby, loped at his heels as he climbed the stairs, and bribed hotel personnel to let them wait for him in his private room. He ran them out at pistol point and directed the house detective to prevent any more such visits if he preferred walking without bullets in his kneecaps. That fellow nodded eager assent; and so Randy was greatly annoyed when within hours of their conversation a fresh knock came to his door.

The small man who greeted him when he tore it open was dressed better than the shabby gentlemen of the press, in a printed yellow waistcoat, striped trousers, velvet lapels, fine boots with tall heels, and a pearl-gray Stetson. His left eye was varnished ivory, with the painted-on iris a shade darker brown than its living mate. He introduced himself as Abraham Cripplehorn, originally of Atlantic City, New Jersey, and in lieu of a calling card presented him with a volume slightly larger than a banker's wallet, bound in scarlet and goldenrod pasteboard and titled:

BRIMSTONE BOB'S REVENGE,
or
GUN JUSTICE IN ABILENE
Being a True and Authentic Account of
Robert Turnstile's Quest for Bloody Vengeance
on the Chisholm Trail.
as told by
JACK DODGER,
an Eye-Witness

"Who's this Jack Dodger, at all?" asked Randy.

"He is I, sir: a *nom de plume,* to spare typesetters the chore of constructing my born appellation. The original Dodger made good on his surname by departing his hotel room in St. Louis, by way of the fire escape, leaving behind an unpaid bill and twenty-five copies of *Petticoat Betsy, the Bandit Princess,* by Jack Dodger. I sold them to a local lending library, which was eager to have them, as Buffalo Bill was appearing locally, and thus financed the rest of my North American tour."

"Which one of these is you?" He pointed to a pen-and-ink drawing on the paper cover of two men in range gear firing pistols at each other at point-blank range, their weapons held out at shoulder length.

"Neither. The fellow on the left is a reasonably accurate likeness of Brimstone Bob Turnstile. His opposing number traveled under the name Creek Morgan until that slug put him six feet under in Kansas. A reputable journalist never places himself in the story."

"I had my fill of writers this day." He started to close the door. A highly polished toe held it open three inches; wide enough for Randy to poke the Colt's muzzle through the space.

Cripplehorn's reaction was to smile under his brush moustache.

"I'm not interested in penning merely another dime novel commemorating a long-standing feud between dangerous men; that would be an expenditure of valuable resources toward too small a reward."

"That's a lot of big words. Which one you want to be your last?" He drew back the hammer.

The visitor was cool in the face of a threat; the reasons behind it I'll go into later and at length. His mission, he explained, was to produce an extravaganza that would pit Randy Locke and Frank Farmer against each other before a paying audience.

"Firing blanks and gibbering like a couple of monkeys in the circus. I ain't interested, and unless Frank's changed since I put a bullet through his chest wall, neither is he."

"I'm not suggesting a Punch-and-Judy show. The arenas

are filled with those. This will be a unique exhibition. A duel to the death."

"The law won't stand for it." But Randy held his fire.

"Allow me to worry about that. There are ways and ways; which is why you need me, and why I am not hesitating to share a valuable idea as this free gratis with a man I've just met. I propose to charge two dollars a head for the privilege of witnessing two genuine frontiersmen engaged in mortal combat; the take to be divided equally between myself and the survivor—or his designated heirs in the event he expires soon after."

"Compared to cash in hand, money in the mouth's worth less than a penny on the dollar."

The man's smile remained as fixed as his ivory eye.

"I'll stand the expense of advertising and promotion. Your only obligation will be to show up on the day, loaded and sober."

"Look around you, Mr. Dodger."

"In informal conversation I prefer Cripplehorn."

"Whatever your name is, look around. This ain't exactly the honeymoon suite in the Bella Union. I'm bust. Gunsmiths don't trade ammunition for tickets to a show."

"I read of your arrival in San Francisco in the telegraph column of *The Chicago Herald*. The fare and accommodations were princely, and I am still awaiting a bank draft from New York City for delivery of my most recent manuscript. I can have a hundred dollars for you in a month."

"I got enough for but two more days, and there ain't no

fire escape. A month from now I'll be back in Wyoming, skinning wolves to eat. You can reach me in Sheridan, care of Western Union. Wire me fifty and we'll talk."

"That's a gamble."

"You saying I can't be trusted?"

"If these past ten years have proven anything, it's that you're a man of your word, Mr. Farmer too. But what if he decides not to cooperate?"

"He will, if it's a chance to get at me."

"The only obstacle," Cripplehorn said, "is the difficulty of locating him."

"If that piece in the paper went out on the wire, he'll come here under his own steam."

"What if one of you kills the other before I can raise the money?"

"It's a fair possibility. Risk like that, I wouldn't want to be in your shoes."

FIVE

Good businessmen are invariably polite, patient, and in step with their customers' best interests.

The intriguing thing about the man who walks in the footsteps of the adventurous is he exposes himself to the same adventures, except in his case with his eyes wide open. Which one is the more courageous and determined, the one who stumbles into hazard or the one who knows of it based on the other's experience and goes on anyway?

Abraham Cripplehorn would hardly have held himself a man of courage. Like any successful salesman, he never bought his own merchandise.

He lost his left eye trying to stay out of the army. Intending to deal himself out of Mr. Lincoln's draft, he took aim at his off foot with an old Paterson, but loaded it with the wrong size ball and it blew up in his face. For a time he wore a piratical patch, but it was anathema to his chosen line of work, which depended on the illusion of comfortable reliability. Blown-glass eyes fell outside the budget of a twenty-year-old entrepreneurial hopeful, but after alighting from a freight in Baltimore he won ten dollars in a game of euchre with a yardman named Tingley, who was short on funds but had an uncle who made pianos. This uncle fashioned an eye from the ivory he used to manufacture keys. It was an improvement over the patch, but the blank white orb still made people feel uncomfortable. With the profits from selling two gold bricks to a naïve postal clerk in Boston, he hired a woman who painted miniatures to add an iris. It didn't fool many people, the color being off a shade, but it made them feel more at ease, and when he told them he'd received the injury at Cold Harbor, it actually worked to his benefit.

"People want to believe a good lie," he said to a companion under the relaxing influence of a bottle of peach brandy, his spirit of choice. "They'll meet you halfway if you show effort in it."

He never repeated the remark. The young man he told it to did, cocking up an enterprise he'd invested a month in preparation, and turned up in a rubbish bin in Pittsburgh with his throat cut. His father, who owned part interest in a coal mine, decided that he'd fallen in with gypsies. Two days later a group of miners attacked a bunch of them in a local camp with pickaxes and burned their tents and wagons. Cripplehorn read about it in a week-old copy of the *Picayune* in a train station in Buffalo, and shook his head.

"Poor rag-headed bastards."

He himself was the son of an Atlantic City plumbing salesman who lived on the road, raised by a succession of aunts who were always coming and going and never seemed to run out of reinforcements. One, who claimed to be a Creole from Louisiana (although he was fairly certain she was Greek, and not the classic variety with a long straight nose and intelligent forehead but a woman with big red hands and a moustache), took his virginity when he was twelve. He thought it was their private secret—illicit lovers sharing a special bond—but after she told his father, describing the cute face little Abie made when he came, the plumbing salesman broke his cheekstrap with a pipe wrench and threw him out of the house.

A neighbor who went to the door to investigate what sounded like a wounded animal moaning on his front porch found him and took him to a doctor, who set the broken bone and put him to rest on a cot in the room behind his office. When the bone had knitted sufficiently for the patient to speak, he said he'd fallen down the back steps of his house, and since his father was on the road with his samples he was on his own. While the doctor was away delivering a baby, Abraham got his clothes from a cupboard, found cash in a tin behind a row of medical journals on a shelf, and crawled into an empty cattle car in the railroad yards, where he fell asleep. When he woke, the world swayed beneath him. He had no idea which way he was headed until the train slowed down approaching the station in Wilmington, Delaware.

Years later, when Abraham had made his way in the world, he traveled back a thousand miles looking for his father with a Stevens shotgun, only to find a granite-and-marble bank sprung up where the house had stood. None of the neighbors remembered anyone of that name. He placed an advertisement in several newspapers, offering a reward for information on the whereabouts of Noah Cripplehorn, with a description. He received nothing but the odd rambling answer from people patently hoping to collect on vagary alone. He gave it up when his money ran out, but he refused to abandon its purpose. As many cities as he visited throughout the years, and as often as he crisscrossed the continent, he never stopped asking after the man, and he kept the scattergun clean and lubricated.

Abraham Cripplehorn never forgot an insult or an injury no matter how slight, and had the patience to wait months or years to even a score.

Stopping in St. Louis in 1872, he got into a scrap with a store clerk over the coloring of a twenty-dollar banknote and cut the man's arm to the bone with a clasp-knife, his preferred weapon of self-defense; he was saving the Stevens for his father. A policeman happened to be present. Cripplehorn came to in a cell with a crusty bump on his head from the officer's nightstick, pleaded guilty to the reduced charge of aggravated assault, and spent six months in the state penitentiary in Jefferson City. His cellmate, an elderly confidence man named Mike Hurly, told him he was wasting his time unloading gold bricks on the gullible and trying to pass counterfeit currency. A young man of his obvious intelligence ought to try his hand at selling trust.

Cripplehorn smiled. "Trust, what's that?"

"Only the difference between going to the customer instead of having him come to you."

"I don't just have the capital right now to rent a storefront."

"I'm talking about personal transactions, not real estate. You can sell pomade to a bald man if you know what you're about."

"That the sound policy that put you in here?"

Hurly's smile was beaming; as opposite to his cell mate's as blue sky to overcast. He was a redheaded Irishman with a nose full of shot veins and ruddy skin pulled all out of shape by a lifetime of beaming. He was thirty-two at the time of their meeting.

"I got drunk celebrating a score and stole a horse and buggy that happened to belong to the mayor of Springfield. It don't count against what I'm telling you."

"Telling or selling?"

"Just now I'm fresh out of merchandise, so you can believe what I'm saying. Under other circumstances I'd be fleecing you out of that Dutch eye. I don't like to see a young man squandering his potential on store clerks without a pot to piss in. How much time you got left?"

"Five months, sixteen days, eleven hours, and change."

"I got another four beyond, on account of I bust that mayor's yellow-wheeled wagon against a telegraph pole misjudging a turn. That's plenty of time to turn you out from Hurly University."

"Does it come with a key I can hang from my watch chain?"

Hurly tapped the other man's chest. "You wear it in there, and it'll open every door this side of St. Peter. Where you go from there depends on what you learn after you leave here."

It was in that cell that Cripplehorn learned the best way to sell a man something he didn't want was to refuse to offer it to him.

He learned also to dress consistently and with dash; nothing so tawdry as a gold tooth, but an article of clothing that set him apart from the bowler-hatted drummer and the sharp in the straw boater. In Jefferson City after his release, he picked a pocket hanging on a peg in a barber shop, bought a readymade suit, and booked a coach to St. Louis. On the platform, a fellow in a cloth cap and mackinaw smoking a cigarette thrust a flyer into his hands, printed in square-serif letters on coarse stock:

OPERA HOUSE!

Friday & Saturday, November 17 & 18

Civilization *v.* Savagery!

Border Perils! Indian Fights!

Performed Right On Stage Before Your Eyes!

BUFFALO BILL!

(W. F. Cody)

TEXAS JACK!

(O.B. Omohundro)

PRINCESS DOVE EYE!

(Mme. G. Morlacchi)

CALE DURG!

(E. Z. C. Judson: "Ned" Buntline)

in

Scouts of The Plains

After a glance he crumpled and threw it into a trash barrel, but was accosted three times on his way to a hotel by similarly attired ruffians bearing identical leaflets, and shook his head at a street peddler offering *cartes d'visites* bearing the photographic likenesses of Cody, Omohundro, Morlacchi, et al; others were not so difficult to persuade, as a small group had gathered on the sidewalk to consider the man's wares.

The hotel was a rattrap, the best he could afford while he considered the business of acquiring *dash.* There he made the acquaintance, by proxy, of one Jack Dodger.

He read *Brimstone Bob's Revenge* in one sitting. When he stood at his window and craned his neck, he could just read the gaslit legend on the marquee of the St. Louis Opera House:

SCOUTS OF THE PLAINS

With what a lending library gave him for the twenty-five copies of Dodger's opus—and it was glad to get it with the Wild West in residence—he bought a better suit and a fine Stetson hat. He hadn't enough to buy a new pair of boots, but at a bootmaker's he procured a pair in glossy black glove leather for the price of resoling, as they'd gone unclaimed by the customer who had brought them in. They pinched his toes, but when he stood before a trifold mirror he decided he could bear them until he could afford a replacement.

By the end of the week, for the small expenditure of a printer's bill, he'd sold enough rolls of tickets at wholesale price to *Scouts of the Plains* to order a pair in his size.

He resisted the temptation, however.

Custom bootmaking takes time, and he had to clear out before the exasperated manager of the opera house set the police looking for the man responsible for two hundred enraged customers who had to be turned away at the door.

When *Scouts of the Plains* closed in San Francisco after a wildly successful tour, William Frederick Cody had become famous. On a smaller scale, it made Abraham Cripplehorn's reputation for disgruntled theater operators all along the circuit, and the only fiction he ever wrote was the names he signed in various hotel registers when Cripplehorn and Dodger were too dangerous to use.

Chicago was always his destination of choice when his pockets sagged with cash. Its pleasures were many and its expectations few. There, in the fall of 1877, he was sitting up in bed in his suite in the Palmer House, eating a princely breakfast and reading the *Sun,* when he first read the names of the Messrs. Locke and Farmer, and saw his way toward a lifetime of the same.

SIX

A man of patience is always content, whereas an impatient man is always suffering from thirst, even when up to his neck in fresh water.

Randy waited for Frank to find him in San Francisco until his money ran out. That process was accelerated by the incentives he'd left among desk clerks in all the likely hotels and porters at the train station to report the arrival of strangers whose ears didn't quite match.

Ten days after his meeting with Abraham Cripplehorn, the situation became untenable. He collected his gear and lit out for wolf country. He wondered if Frank had come to grief; wondered it with a touch of concern, as if he'd lost someone close.

Frank, however, had lost nothing but his touch with current affairs.

He was back in Colorado, working for the territorial

stock-growers' association, armed with a Remington rolling-block rifle his employers had charged against his first month's wages, riding fence for all the big ranches and discouraging rustlers; which was a term loose enough to cover a variety of pests, most often small-time ranchers who represented an obstacle to progress.

The small-fry countered the pressure by forming an association of their own and sending delegates to Denver, but the courts there and eventually the governor ruled against them on the grounds that nearly all of the complainants had paid a fine or served time for cattle theft.

Neither the members of the bench nor the governor had worked in the trade. They could not be made to see that every spread, the large ones included, had begun with someone swinging a wide loop. The big fish had just gotten there first, before there was a badge to intervene or a capital to try the case.

Although Frank was not offered a badge, he and his fellow designates upheld the law as set forth in the Denver decisions, and assumed the added responsibilities of judge and jury, pronouncing and carrying out sentences of death on the spot. It was a question of arithmetic, and of simple economics: a citizen's arrest, followed by a trek of a week or more to the nearest district court, with at least three men to guard the prisoners and two to give testimony. With cases already backed up into next year, months went by with the ranches short-handed. A rifle in the right hands served the same purpose in less than a second.

"What we fixing to call these fellows?" asked one beef baron, smoking a cigar in a silver holder to keep from staining his white beard with tobacco.

A short silence followed among those gathered in the association's club room. A baron with an ear trumpet broke it.

"Regulators. Seeing as how we're paying top-hand wages to return things to regular."

The pay was good, no question, but it might have been Confederate scrip for all it was useful four months out of the year, apart from stuffing his shirt and waistcoat to keep out the infernal cold. Frank spent his first winter in a dugout line shack built into a foothill in the San Miguels, bark logs in front and the rest dirt. When he wasn't snowed in, he patrolled a region the size of a European duchy, going weeks without seeing a white man. The only newspapers he saw were months old, left behind by the shack's previous occupant to start fires, and the circumstances of his employment prevented him from pumping drifters for information about the world outside. Those he came across were where they shouldn't be; he shot them out from under their hats when he could, or else kicked up a clump of snow at their feet that sent them over the nearest ridge lickety-split.

The Indians he saw—stragglers off the reservation—were too wily to come within rifle range, much less offer conversation; in any case, they were unlikely to be abreast of what was going on in California, or for that matter the moon.

It was a bad winter, and spring was worse. He could hear the ice breaking up above the treeline, the noise like dynamiters blasting tunnels for the railroad, and the rumble of avalanches. When after one ten-day circuit he couldn't find the shack, he knew it was gone, pounded flat as a griddle under tons of snow and rock. He reckoned then it was time to return to civilization.

Two days' ride from ranch headquarters he spotted Juan Valiente, a fellow Regulator, cutting west from the Animas. He recognized his deep-chested dun first, then the man himself by the elaborate moustaches he wore in a hammock when he slept to keep them tame. Frank didn't like him, having lost friends and a good horse to men who looked like him near the Rio Grande, but he saved his strongest emotions for someone else. They drew alongside each other, the dun facing north, Frank's gray pointed south, the mounts' breath mingling in a cloud thick as custard.

"Any?" asked Valiente.

"One. Three more still running, I reckon. You?"

"I shot a boy."

"How old?"

The Mexican shrugged, the elegance of the gesture inherited from conquerors in brass hats.

"*Diez y tres,* maybe. Maybe fourteen. That skinning knife it made him older."

"Sure he had it on him when you shot him?"

Valiente shrugged again.

"Got paper for rolling?"

"Just the newspaper. Warmer than longjohns." Valiente reached inside his bearskin and pulled out a thick fold of newsprint.

Apparently the Mexican burned as he read, having smoked his way through all the pieces about schoolteachers running off with their students and illustrated advertisements for ladies' foundation garments, leaving only telegraph columns and optimistic predictions for the wheat harvest. Frank was tearing out a square when an item caught his eye:

> *San Francisco, Mar. 16*—It has come to our editors' attention that Mr. Randolph Locke, the Notorious Texas pistoleer, is visiting our city, and at last word was stopping at the Eldorado Hotel. . . .

The range manager's wife, a tall woman who dipped snuff, kept the books. She worked for wages same as Frank, but she gave up every company penny like she was passing a kidney stone.

"Rebuilding a line shack takes time. I ought to take it out of yours."

"You already did. I lost some gear when the mountain fell on top of it."

"A man should know better than to shoot during a thaw. It brings landslides."

"It's what you pay me for, only I'm still waiting."

"I sometimes wonder who is costing us more, you gun men or the dirty cattle thieves."

He was gone an hour when a rider caught up with him. The sheriff, a German named Dierdorf, said he had to take him in for threatening the range manager's wife with a revolver.

"I just showed it to her, asking where I could get the grips replaced."

"That is too thin for me."

"First they hire me to stop the stealing, then they try stealing from me. What do you do when a man goes to robbing you—or a woman, comes to that?"

"*Verdammt!* I had a dog mean as her I'd feed it to a grizzly, but I work for the association same as you. I got to take you to town."

"I'm late as it is, by about three months. Tell her you missed me."

Dierdorf sighed and laid the muzzle of his horse pistol alongside Frank's temple.

Sixty days, said the judge in Denver.

The shinplasters called the wolf White Ike, but the only thing white about him was his muzzle, and as to Ike, whoever put up the bounty had probably had an uncle by that name nobody liked. Anyway it looked good with a five-hundred-dollar bounty printed under the description and a woodcut illustration that looked as if it had been done by a child.

Randy had come all the way to the top of Montana Territory to answer the flyer he'd seen in Billings; what with tracking a trail that doubled back and crossed itself like a crazy man on a bicycle, and blizzards wiping out even that, he wasn't sure but that he was in Canada.

White Ike was one of those aged loners, cast out of the pack by some young whelp with faster reflexes and the itch to lead, who'd gotten shrewd in order to survive on his own. He sprang traps by kicking dirt and snow on them, gobbled the bait, and picked off stray calves not yet learned in the ways of self-preservation, at a rate that had placed his likeness in store windows and on barn walls alongside wanted murderers. The men who gathered in saloons in broad daylight claimed he'd developed a taste for babies and came down from the mountains to climb through windows and snatch them from their cradles, but those were stories told to tenderheels for the price of a shot of Old Gideon. Nothing he'd heard about wolves attacking humans had stood up under close questioning.

On the other hand, creatures left on their own took on ways no man could predict. This he knew from personal experience.

Anyhow, it was all the same to him, and better, if it hiked the bounty. Wolfing was going the way of buffalo running;

all Randy had to show for the season was a couple of moth-eaten pelts he'd peeled off starved carcasses and some coyote skins he'd tried to pass off as the real thing and gotten himself run out of Helena for the trouble. He was down to his last half-pound of bacon and an elk quarter that had commenced to spoil. He'd carved off what he could for jerking before the stink made his eyes water, but he was loath to shoot another. Crossing the Missouri near Fort Benton, his horse had spooked when a hawser snapped in two, capsized the ferry, and dumped them both into the water. The ferryman had swum to shore and Randy, too, but his horse was last seen treading water on the way to Great Falls with his pack aboard. He was down to the cartridges on his belt, and he wasn't too sure of all of them after that soaking. After he shot Ike, he'd take his chances on the rest for meat. Then he'd shoot the mule he'd traded for at a ranch. It was hardy enough, but it had to be beaten with a rope-end to get started.

He was carrying his Colt and his old Circle X Ballard rifle, its stock scratched many times over with pawnbrokers' identifying marks. He wasn't the hand with a long gun Frank was, but if you got close enough to an animal like Ike to shoot it with a revolver, you might as well sprinkle its tail with salt.

He was close now, he could tell. The wolf kept climbing, headed for the treeline, where prey was scarce. It knew it was being followed. Its best hope was to draw him far enough from his own kind to even the odds.

Randy smiled at that. Even a smart wolf was too dumb to count, and too ignorant of his pursuer's situation to know he lived his life far from his own kind.

He was thinking these thoughts, when what he ought to be thinking about was wolf only, when snow squeaked and he turned and looked up in time to see two rows of fangs and red mouth surrounded by a halo of pale muzzle and two sets of claws streaking his way, the whole foreshortened against blue sky, as if it had dropped from a hot-air balloon: the drop a good sixty feet straight down from a rocky outcrop square above Randy's head. He could feel the heat of the animal's desperate breath when he stuck the Ballard straight up and fired.

A Cheyenne dog soldier named Bending Bough found them, so tangled together he thought at first he'd discovered one of the half-men-half-beasts of tribal legend. After he sorted them out he treated the man's frightening wounds with mud and dried herbs, fed him soup made from White Ike's liver, and brought him across the back of the mule to the nearest settlement.

It was a place of clapboard and canvas, hanging by its fingernails to the side of a mountain the settlers were systematically hollowing out in search of a vein of silver that came and went like a broken line on a map. Everything appeared to be held together by soot, including the miners. The rigorous toil and inescapable filth had made them surly and suspicious of strangers, particularly those who came in strange colors.

Bending Bough tried to pass as the wounded man's guide and sell the dead wolf's pelt, but the Indian had gotten himself as confused as Randy, thinking himself in Canada: It was Montana, and the locals considered any red men coming from the north to be fugitives from justice following the Little Big Horn massacre. The mercantile owner to whom he'd offered the pelt sent word to the citizens' committee, who hanged the Indian in the livery stable. For a time, Randy was kept under guard in a back room of the assayer's office as a suspected turncoat, his wounds tended by a barber who was the closest thing the town had to a medical man, but when he was well enough to give an account of himself they argued over the matter, then decided one hanging would hold them for a while. They loaded him aboard his mule, aimed it south, and gave it a hard smack. White Ike's pelt stayed behind, to be sold and the five hundred divided among the miners.

•

SEVEN

In order to speak to a lady for the first time, an introduction is required, either by a relative or by a mutual acquaintance if no relative is available.

After he was voted out of office on account of age and deafness and he was left all on his own, Gunter Dierdorf didn't blame his widowed state for his loneliness, nor his daughter's desertion, nor even Frank Farmer, who had probably hastened his wife's death and certainly had deprived him of his only child. If there was one mortal soul in this world he hated—hated as much as Frank and Randy hated each other—it was Morris Fassbinder, professor emeritus from the Utica College of Engineering. If the old gentleman was still living and wandered inside range of the sawed-off Greener the sheriff had carried throughout his tenure and which now hung above the stone fireplace in his retirement shack, the burial service would need Mason jars.

If a man had to be incarcerated, he could have done worse than the jailhouse in the county seat where Frank served out his two months for persuading the range manager's wife to pay him what he'd earned as a Regulator. The cells were clean, the sheets laundered and placed on a real bed (iron thing, might have been built from a cemetery fence, with a ditch down the middle of the mattress, but a bed just the same), and a lamp provided for reading the week-old newspapers from Denver after the sheriff was through with them. The meals were bland—Mrs. Dierdorf skimped on salt, which was not included in the official budget—but they were hot and never undercooked, and best of all they came in a picnic basket covered with a checked cloth hung on the slender arm of Evangeline Dierdorf.

The sheriff's daughter had attended a presentation by Doctor the Professor Morris Fassbinder in the Masonic Hall, a major stop on the Chautauqua lecture circuit originating in New York State. The elderly scholar, a scarecrow in a clawhammer coat, stiff collar, hard black hat, pinch-nose spectacles, long white hair, and dandruff, had served on the parole board in Elmira, and circumnavigated the country pressing for prison reform.

"Contrary to conventional belief," he told his audiences, "unfortunates placed under lock and key for their offenses against the statutes are not there to be punished or reformed, but rather for storage. Society simply does not know what to do with them, and so when the offense is not of a capital nature it shelves them out of sight, and too frequently out of mind. When they have paid their debt, what course is left to them but to return to old habits? They offend, they are captured, tried, and placed once again on that remote shelf, to begin the process all over again when they are released.

"Surely a Christian nation can do better. . . ."

The Fassbinder System (as it was advertised in playbills and on a large pasteboard sign propped on an easel downstage) involved humane treatment for these overlooked individuals. It was based upon the parable of the Good Samaritan, and although it offered no guarantee that he who was done unto as others would have done unto them would pass along the favor, the present system of penalty through neglect was a virtual promise that the cycle would repeat itself "*ad infinitum, ad absurdum,* world without end."

The lecture came with statistics demonstrating the sad percentage of recidivism as it stood, and projected figures based on the professor's exhaustive studies of the behavior of certain wild animals kept in captivity and the docility of those that were provided with a healthy diet, their cages cleaned regularly, and treated overall with patience and kindness, as opposed to those that were not. (This part of the programme was the only one wherein the speaker referred to notes printed in his neat hand on three-by-five cards; the fact that the projected figures were his own invention did not impose itself upon the mesmeric rhythms of his sentences or the melodiousness of his voice.)

"Surely"—his favorite adverb—"a man built in God's

image and a woman fashioned from the First Man's costal cartilage, whatever his or her transgressions, is worthy of the same gentle treatment as a bear or a lion."

Evangeline was impressed, as much by the presenter's erect bearing and sonorous tenor as by his central theme, and returned to her parents' home from the evening with her handsome head filled with ideas about reading lamps, clean sheets, and good food delivered with a charitable word and a sweet smile. The sheriff and his wife doted on their daughter, whose three siblings had died in infancy. The elder Dierdorfs never stood a chance: The reforms were put into effect.

Moreover, she was a graceful creature, long-necked, with a high intelligent brow, a straight nose, agreeably curved lips, and a waist a man's two hands could encompass without effort. Her eyes were brown, clear, and required no spectacles to see that the prisoner was a man pleasingly formed (his artificial ear brought sympathy for his unfortunate past rather than revulsion), clean in his habits, and sufficiently well-bred to rise when a lady approached his cell.

Evangeline Dierdorf was twenty-two when Frank Farmer walked out of that cell a free man and ran away with her to Denver.

The couple did not remain long in that town.

Although Frank considered that the sheriff would not be long in tracing them (he arrived a week later), that eventuality didn't bother him so much as the time that had elapsed since the last news of Randy. He was still carrying around the piece he'd torn out of the newspaper in Colorado, worn gossamer thin and the print nearly rubbed away from taking out and rereading. It was too much to hope his enemy was still in San Francisco, but that was the place to start looking. Randy's new notoriety would certainly leave a trail in the memories of those who had encountered him.

Evangeline was thrilled. The delights of Denver, piled atop the discovery of her body, were sufficient to spin the head of a sheltered young lady; the City on the Bay had always seemed as far away and as drenched in romance as Mecca.

With Evangeline's life savings, together with what he got from selling his horse and the long-range rifle, Frank booked a coach to the coast. But long before the train rolled into the station he grew weary of the company, and slipped away in the confusion of people on the platform. Evangeline spent the rest of the money she'd brought on hotels she got little good from, wandering the streets most of the time hoping to glimpse Frank, then dropped out of the lives of all who knew her. Scant months later, a woman answering her description was found in a rented flat overlooking the railroad tracks in Carson City, Nevada, dead of an overdose of laudanum, and buried in an unmarked grave in potter's field. The local marshal was a former deputy of Gunter Dierdorf's. The Colorado sheriff, wearing a mourning band for his recently deceased wife, came in person to arrange for the disinterment, identification, and transportation home.

On the day Frank had arrived, a loafer holding up the porch over the platform with his shoulders saw a man threading his way through the crowd, moving on the double. He passed close enough for the loafer to spot his gutta-percha ear.

He hadn't seen the man who'd promised him a reward for that information in months; but if it was worth something to him, the fact that he was interested in that ear might be worth something to the man who wore it. He pushed his dirty hat determinedly forward to his eyebrows and followed on the man's heels. On the way he passed a pretty young woman with a parasol, anxiously peering around herself in the middle of the throng. He hesitated, sensing an errand there, and pocket money in it, then resumed his pursuit of the man with the ear, shaking his head. It was either drought or downpour in his work.

Frank went first to the Eldorado Hotel, but the desk clerk couldn't find Randy Locke in the current register. Further inquiries led finally to his last-known stop in town, in a hotel not reputed for its elegance, equipped with roaches the size of cigar butts, two sheets of wallpaper separating each room from its neighbor, and a woman's false eyelash stuck to the basin in the dry-sink. He thought he could smell Randy on the sheets; which may not have been pure fancy on his part. For three days he lay on the bed his old acquaintance had slept on, hoping to draw intelligence from the contact; but apart from the attention of bedbugs he drew nothing from the experience.

"I was glad to see the last of him," said the manager, contemplating a bale of hair he'd plucked from a nostril. "He was starting to attract reporters."

"Any other visitors?"

The manager dislodged the hair from his fingers onto his lapel, staring at Frank. Frank stuck a banknote across the desk.

"One-eyed jasper in a ten-gallon hat."

Frank got out another banknote. The manager looked at it regretfully and said he never got the man's name. His guest checked out.

"Frank Farmer?"

He spun, dropping his valise and dragging the worn revolver from its holster.

"Steady, feller!" A man wearing a dirty coat and dirtier plug hat stood on the boardwalk with his hands in the air.

"How'd you know my name?"

"When somebody says there's money in it, I ain't likely to forget it, nor the name of the one offering."

"Well?"

"Feller called Locke."

"When?"

"A spell back. Last fall it was."

"That's no good to me."

"Maybe no, maybe yes; but it was right there in that hotel I talked to him. There's generally always somebody needs some sort of favor in places like it. I make it a point to keep it on my rounds."

"I already know he stayed there."

"What you don't know's the name of the man I seen coming down from his room before that. Had him on good boots and a pretty hat. I asked him if he needed any errands run. He gave me a dollar and told me to bring him a bottle of peach brandy at the Palace. This here's what he gave me instead of cash when I showed up with it," he said bitterly. "I been carrying it since I seen you at the station. You lost me, but I reckoned you'd turn up here sooner than later."

Frank looked at the scuffed cover of the book the loafer had pulled from his hip pocket:

BRIMSTONE BOB'S REVENGE,

or

GUN JUSTICE IN ABILENE

Being a True and Authentic Account of
Robert Turnstile's Quest for Bloody Vengeance
on the Chisholm Trail

as told by

JACK DODGER,

an Eye-Witness

"Who's this Turnstile?"

"Never heard of 'em, nor Dodger neither. He said it wasn't even his name."

"What was?"

The loafer grinned at him. Frank grunted and fished out another banknote.

EIGHT

A firm handshake and a pleasant way of speaking are the working capital of the successful businessman.

Abraham Cripplehorn was suffering the longest string of bad luck of his career.

He laid it to Jack Dodger.

The elusive Jack had always been his rabbit's foot: Those copies of *Petticoat Betsy, the Bandit Princess* he'd found in his hotel room had brought direction to an aimless life, but the association had not been so rosy for The Mercury Press of Cincinnati, Ohio, which had declared bankruptcy in 1876, leaving five hundred copies of *Brimstone Bob's Revenge* unclaimed at its printer's. Cripplehorn had happened upon this information while visiting that city, and had obtained them by settling the bill. When he gave the last one to a St. Louis theater manager he'd hoped to persuade to advance him money against a public duel to the death between Randy Locke and Frank Farmer, his fortunes turned sour.

The manager, who'd demanded time to think over his proposition, turned him down the next day, and he was ejected from his hotel at the end of the week for nonpayment, minus his luggage. In due course he found himself in an establishment not unlike the one where he'd met Locke, and after he pawned his silver pocket watch to finance his stay there, he faced the fact that the street would be his next place of lodging if something didn't happen soon to reverse his situation.

Walking around the block to consider the matter, he stopped on a corner to wait for a brewer's dray to pass and read an engraved brass plaque attached to the four-story brick building at his elbow:

REDEMPTION HOUSE

Not being one to fail to recognize an opportunity or an omen, he climbed the front steps and rang the bell. A woman in black bombazine with her hair in a bun answered, frowning at his gaudy waistcoat, high-heeled boots, and dramatic hat brim.

"Pray, madam, what is the nature of this establishment?"

The woman adjusted her rimless spectacles. "We are a charitable institution affiliated with the First Unitarian Church. Our ambition is to reform the drunkard and close the temple of blue ruin for good and all."

He let fall his crest. "I took it for a pawnshop. Do you know of one in this neighborhood?"

"Certainly not." She began to close the door.

He plucked out his ivory eye and held it up. "I intended to barter this for the price of that blue ruin you mentioned; but perhaps it was the Lord, and not my infernal thirst, that led me to your door."

Which thereupon opened wide.

For an incentive, the desk clerk at the Palace Hotel brought out an old registration book from the back room and found a forwarding address for Abraham Cripplehorn: The Palmer House, Chicago. Frank cursed his luck, and while he was at it Sheriff Gunter Dierdorf and the range manager's wife in Colorado. His money wouldn't cover the cost of a wire to ask if the man was registered there, much less a trip that far east; and even if it would, he'd sooner spend it looking for Randy direct.

In any case, the fellow might be just a chance acquaintance. There was no surety he knew something Frank didn't.

The desk clerk said, "You might try your luck around November. Mr. Cripplehorn often spends the winter in San Francisco, and he always stays here."

Frank thanked him for the information. November was three months off; but what was that against the years he'd put in already? It wasn't as if he hadn't another pursuit to occupy him in the meantime.

Cripplehorn was a gifted speaker. He'd discovered the fact in Deadwood, where a run of cards no one quite accepted as accidental had forced him to talk his way out of a short rope and a long drop. Not long after in St. Paul, Minnesota, when his capital was almost as low as at present, he'd stepped in at the last moment for a lecturer on personal hygiene who'd been detained for lewd and lascivious conduct. He'd sent the male half of the audience in the Gaiety Theatre running for the nearest bathhouse with his tale of a Union infantryman whose masculine member had fallen off at Gettysburg for lack of attention to the foreskin.

The ladies of Redemption House, once they'd obtained his pledge never again to partake of strong drink, asked him to address the congregation at the First Unitarian Church, laying open his sordid story and assigning the credit for his reform to the efforts of the organization; for there is a little of the confidence man in us all, when everything's said and done. No remuneration was offered, but when some twenty of his listeners came forward after the final hymn to sign the Pledge, a charter member of the charitable society pressured her husband, a booking agent for Chautauqua, to send him on tour with a salary and all expenses paid. (Coincidentally, he shared his first bill, in Des Moines, Iowa, with Dr. Morris Fassbinder, that well-known advocate for a humane penal system.)

His narrative always started out gently, as if in private conversation. When he came to his sad, riveting story, his voice fell to a murmur, as if he hoped to obscure the shameful details. (His listeners, in fact, were forced to lean forward in their seats and strain their ears during this portion of the address, and therefore captured every word.) Finally he built to a proud and powerful annunciation of his faith in the Lord and the dramatically improved situation that had come of finding Him.

He used just enough of his own story—the spoliation of his innocence, his father's pipe wrench, the horrors of the road—to lend weight to the presentation; he left out evading Mr. Lincoln's draft as impolitic, assigning his injury to an alcohol-influenced incident during army training leading to a medical discharge. The rest of it he'd drawn from a slim volume he found in a bookshop in Cincinnati, purporting to be the privately published confessions of its author. The low point—his attempt to trade his artificial eye for temporary oblivion—was the most popular feature. In time it came to consume the greater part of his oratory. It was his *East Lynne.*

He had a rich tenor, pleasing to men and women both (although to a greater degree in the case of women), which he obtained by seasoning his vocal cords backstage with a pull at a flask filled with peach brandy. In lecture halls, tents, open-air arenas, and melodeons from the Ohio Valley to the High Sierras, the Hon. Abraham Titus Cripplehorn (he added the Titus halfway through the circuit, assuring himself two lines in the playbills), Deacon of the First Unitarian Church of Cincinnati, Ohio, and the Voice of

Redemption House, railed against the devil in the bottle, shared in the box office proceeds, and put away a little each week to finance the extravaganza he regarded as the venture that would allow him to retire to a lifetime of presidential suites and champagne cocktails.

The tour finished in San Francisco, just in time for winter.

"Mr. Cripplehorn?"

He turned from the register in the onyx-and-marble lobby of the Palace Hotel, expecting a word of praise from an attendant of his lectures, and found himself facing a long-legged man in a town suit that despite recent brushing had absorbed more than its share of dust, sweat, and wood smoke, with a sunburn that looked as if it went all the way to the underside of his skin. He had a pink left ear and visible traces of wax where it had been attached.

NINE

Winter: when Mother Nature doffs her bright autumn fashions and dons soft white flannel.

"Cookie, your right name's Locke, ain't it?"

Randy was fishing for a fly that had dropped into his kettle of stew. "Who's asking?"

"Hell, it's me, Shorty. We been in the same bunkhouse near a year now."

"You're all Shorty or Slim or Stretch or Simp. All of you start with *S* and you all got the same jug ears and monkey face. I stopped trying to cut you out a long time ago."

He'd been working on the Lazy Y spread in Nebraska since last fall; his predecessor, also called Cookie, had confused loco weed with wild asparagus, took a taste, saw a thousand Sioux mounted on ten-foot ponies, and run smack-dab into the smokehouse stone wall, breaking his neck.

"It's a big outfit," said the foreman, a man as brown and

wrinkled as a tobacco pouch made from buffalo scrotum. "Think you can feed it?"

"I already got a leg up over the last. I hate asparagus."

And now this.

"Well, is it Locke or ain't it?" Shorty pressed. "Rudolph, right?"

He cornered the fly against a floating piece of bacon fat, scooped it up with the wooden spoon, flung it back over his shoulder, and stirred the stew with the spoon. "Randolph. I'm Randy to foremen and better. Mr. Locke to you rannies."

"Sandy Ross bet me a cartwheel dollar you're the Locke shot a fellow named Farmer in Texas and again in Utah."

"He left out Kansas."

"You saying you're him?"

He said nothing, concentrating. One fly generally led to another.

"What'd he do to you, you wanted him in the ground all this time? He steal your girl or what?"

"Why steal 'em? You can't trade 'em later for a saddle."

"Well, then, what?"

"Don't like him."

"I don't much like Sandy, but we don't go gunning for each other."

"You never met Frank."

"You're fooling me. You're no pistolero. That leg of yours always gets into camp five minutes after the rest of you. Why is it all you cookies are stove up?"

"What whole man wants to shake out while the rooster's still snoring and get a fire going just to keep a bunch of worthless tramps from starving to death?"

"Aw, you're full of sheepdip. Do I get that buck out of Sandy or what? I—"

Before the stubble-face cowhand could react, Randy swept his Colt out from under his bloodstained apron, cocked it, and sped a slug past his left ear.

"You're lucky you ain't Frank. I took that same ear clean off with just a chamber pot."

Randy hadn't the born talents of a chef. He was a good enough man with a skillet or a kettle, and his coffee was strong without being bitter, but he could never find tracks in a biscuit. They always came out burned on the bottom and doughy inside, and as a hot biscuit smeared with lard was the first thing a man sank his teeth into on the range, the men of the Lazy Y began each day out of sorts. But when the story of what happened to Shorty Cochran got around, they stopped griping.

The world was turning still, faster west of St. Louis. The Comanches had been whipped in Texas, Sitting Bull was a federal prisoner, and the only hostiles anyone had seen lately outside Apache country were the ones who had chased the last cookie into the smokehouse wall. Abilene was closed to cows and cowboys. People were roller-skating in Dodge City. When the Lazy Y sent its beef to market, the drive ended after two miles, where the bawling Herefords were loaded aboard the cars in Lincoln. If the tourists didn't waste their money on silver belt buckles shaped like longhorns, Randy might have forgotten what the flea-bitten bastards looked like. Homesteaders were fencing the open range into little-bitty squares where hogs rooted and sugar beets swoll up in the ground the buffalo had trod hard as iron, cutting off the cattle outfits from water. In the last year alone, the Bar 9 in Wyoming and the Double Diamond in New Mexico had broken up and sold all their equipment at auction; every time the wind blew east, it brought with it another dusty band of hands looking for work that wasn't there. A man got up in the dark to heat up his Dutch oven and when it got dark again he didn't know if there'd be a ranch still there in the morning.

Then came winter, and it was all gone in a season.

September and October were mild, more like spring than autumn. The grass stayed slick and green, and the syndicate based in Indiana that owned the Lazy Y was considering expanding next year and taking over acreage belonging to smaller competitors less equipped to weather the changes in the industry. Christmas was snowless, the sky scraped clean of clouds; Randy put on his mackinaw to start breakfast and by the time it was served had shucked it off, the lining sodden with sweat. On New Year's Eve, those hands who'd drawn the short straws and stayed home from Lincoln and its saloons sat outside around a fire, pouring whiskey into their tin cups and passing the bottle. At midnight, under a sky punched through with stars and a three-quarter moon as bright as a new Morgan dollar, one of them produced a firecracker from his shirt pocket; the explosion set the horses rustling in their stalls and left behind a stench of brimstone.

Around 1:00 A.M. someone drew a gray sheet overhead and wrung out a drizzle that rattled against the galvanized iron roof of the bunkhouse like bits of shattered crystal. An hour later the sleet became snow: big, downy, wet flakes at first, floating aimlessly and sizzling when they touched down, then turning to powder, coming faster, swept along by a mad coyote wind from the north whose howling drowned out the panes rattling in their frames. Standing at the windows, staring out between hammocks of white in the corners into the leaden dawn, the hands of the Lazy Y could not know how many others were doing the same at that moment, in a line of bunkhouses stretching from as far up as Dakota to as far down as southeast Texas, and from the bootjack of the Platte in northern Colorado to St. Louis. Somewhere in the heavens a massive flour sifter moved from west to east, dumping two feet of powder over drift fences and buffalo wallows, and behind it a bellows blew it into eight-foot drifts, obliterating sharp contrasts in the earth's surface and smoothing it all into a gently undulating mass dense as fresh-poured cement.

A peaceful sight, when the storm ran out of steam after three days and three nights; until a rider kicking his horse through chest-deep snow moved from solid earth to a hidden swale and found himself buried to the crown of his hat, or a herd of cattle bunched together tight for the heat and froze, to be found still standing in a stiff mass of a hundred when the snows receded in the tragic spring. The mercury dropped to twenty below and ran out of thermometer at the bottom. Cottonwoods burst from the relentless contraction. Locomotives and the string of cars behind them stood motionless, their wheels invisible so that they appeared to have been abandoned unfinished, only the smoke from their stacks showing any sign of activity as their firemen struggled to keep the boilers from cooling and cracking apart. Wood parties wrapped in bearskins and mackinaws trudged out in snowshoes and brought back frozen limbs that snapped and spat as they thawed in the flames and sometimes put out the fire with the sudden release of water. The mail could not go through and the telegraph wires were down, so the men of the Lazy Y couldn't know the situation was the same in Waco and Wichita, Rochester and Rapid City.

The cattle that didn't freeze died of starvation and thirst; thirst, with snow to their chins because the knot-headed beasts didn't know it was frozen water and could be eaten. A schoolgirl outside Omaha didn't return home from school and her body was located when someone spotted a green hair ribbon almost buried in snow, a hundred yards from her house. A Lazy Y cowboy named Shag, nineteen years old and in good health, burst his heart trying to get hay to a stranded herd across four miles of drift; his snow-blind horse was found helpless beside his body, the pallet of feed behind it, still tethered to its saddle. The ground was too hard to bury him, and so a rick of wood was moved in order to get to the insulated earth beneath.

Randy Locke kept his fire stoked all day and all night, feeding the hands as they straggled in to refuel, change horses, and then go back out, trying to contain the damage. No one complained about his biscuits.

Three hundred died, some homesteaders frozen in their shacks when firewood ran out and all the furniture had been broken up to feed the hearths. It was futile to attempt to count the cattle that had perished; the original inventories were based on speculation, much of it over-optimistic; few had any idea of how many they had in the fall, but could guess at how many they had in the spring; they were that easy to count now. Teams of workhorses hauled tons of rotting carcasses into buffalo wallows and covered the common graves to prevent plague. Wolves, at least, found an advantage. With meat available for the picking in greater amounts than any since buffalo days, the packs swelled. An experienced wolfer could make a fortune—if only there were any big ranchers left to pay the bounty.

The blizzards of the 1880s ended the open range—without debate, and almost without complaint; those immediately affected had already shouted themselves hoarse against un-maternal Mother Nature. Fences were required to keep the herds from drifting before the blasting winds, away from ranch headquarters and moving with the storm rather than out of it. The annoyance of it was having to stop every couple of miles and open a gate. The tragedy of it was looking out on a land once untamed, now cut into squares like a pan of dowdy, and proud, sprawling feudal estates gone on the block.

"Where do you go from here, Cookie?" The foreman with the wrinkled brown skin of a scrotum tobacco pouch counted out his wages from the scratched green strongbox on the butcher-block table he used for a desk.

"Where do you?" He scooped the banknotes into his sweaty old hat and swept it onto his head swiftly, to avoid spilling; it was like flipping a flapjack.

"Hartford, Connecticut. My daughter's been after me to move in with her and her husband since I turned fifty. She's scared I'll fall off my horse and bust my hip. You got any kin?"

"I had a brother. He was born dead, with two heads. They got him in a jar of alcohol in a museum in Michigan. I don't allow as he's much company. I reckon I'll turn west and keep on riding till my bones thaw if ever."

"How old are you?"

"Thirty-six or -seven. Nobody ever wrote down the date that I know of. They probably thought I'd wind up in a jar myself."

The foreman chuckled, working the rheumatism out of

his knuckles. "Your bones'll thaw, don't you worry about that. You figure Texas?"

"Nothing for me there. San Francisco. I got enough to put me up in something better than that bug hatchery I was in last time."

TEN

True friends are always close, no matter the distance that separates them.

The West was a big place, sure enough; but not yet settled. There was a relative handful of lively venues where a rootless man could find work or fun or both, so it was never a coincidence when two men who knew each other well kept crossing paths. While it was true a visitor to New York City, stacked twelve-deep as it was so that when someone came in from outside someone else was pushed out to make room for him, could spend a winter there without ever bumping into an old acquaintance, Tombstone and Fort Griffin and even a sprawl like St. Louis weren't any of them big enough to get lost in.

Randy Locke, however, had managed to step square off the face of the earth.

Wires to ranches in all the places he and Frank had worked came to nothing, beyond a tinhorn gambler going by the name of R. Lockwood, who'd been drug bare naked through mescal outside Las Vegas, New Mexico, from slipping up and dealing two queens of clubs during a friendly game in the Bloody Dog Saloon; but that hideless fellow didn't sound like Randy, who'd been known to cheat himself inadvertently in a game of Patience and invest his last ten dollars in the cowhands' Christmas fund as a self-imposed fine. Frank submitted that Randy was made out of honester clay than he himself.

It was as obvious as finding a trout in one's whiskey that he was out wolfing, which was solitary work and anonymous, encompassing a piece of North America roughly the size of western Europe, with parts as big as the Hebrides that no two could agree on as to their topographical nature. The rangy critters had got cagy of late, withdrawing higher into the mountains and deeper into the wilderness, where a man's footprint in the fallen pine needles was as rare as a whorehouse blush. Frank reckoned he'd have to wait for the thaw for the old thorn in his side to fester out.

(As it happened, Randy had come down from the mountains almost a year earlier, joining the Lazy Y in the middle of its last true trail drive after its cookie brained himself escaping phantom hostiles, relieving the boy who scrubbed his frying pans of his temporary promotion; such brevet appointments rarely reached the general record, and even the foreman scratched his head over Cookie's right name.)

Frank meanwhile took work as an officer for the local Committee of Public Vigilance, breaking up dens of vice and corruption in that part of San Francisco known as the

Barbary Coast. The committee, headed up by clergy and the respected sons of forty-niners, was sworn to beat out the vermin like trod-down dirt from a very old rug, in the interest of saving the city from the whole reason their fathers had come to it in the first place. When an establishment known for entertaining certain pleasures came under special scrutiny—an heir dead of too much opium here, an old reprobate vanished through a trapdoor into the bay there—whereupon he metamorphosed into "an elderly gentleman fallen upon difficulties beyond bearing"—Frank went in with a squad of "reserve officers of the Metropolitan Police" and, armed with truncheons, brass knuckles, and bulldog pistols, cleaned the place out of everything fragile, portable, and potable. It was volunteer duty, paying only in the warmth of the Lord's work well-fulfilled and whatever collateral benefits resulted. Frank sold half a dozen cases of confiscated skullbender the day after his first raid, and paid off his bill outstanding at the Hotel de Paris with change to spare. The next week, he led a raid on the establishment that had bought it, reclaimed half what he'd sold along with a case of genuine French champagne (bottled in San Diego), and sold it next day to the Bella Union, with a tinge of regret; the proprietor was a large contributor to the vigilance committee, and enjoyed a clean bill as a consequence.

These were palmy days for Frank. A man could do the Lord's work, and be comfortable in the bargain. He only regretted he hadn't seen the light years earlier.

On his third week on duty came a revelation.

In a hovel built entirely from wrecked ships—ancient barnacles clinging to the timbers looking like dried-up onions—an old Chinaman, himself built entirely from burlap stretched over weathered canvas, a rusty black mandarin's cap pasted to his skull, looked up at the intruders with a butcher's cleaver clutched in one hand, stained with something that was not rust. A young Chinese woman whom it developed was his daughter lay at his slippered feet with her head nearly clean off her body. As Frank reconstructed the situation, she had taken up with a twenty-year-old white man, scion of a fortune struck in '49 or thereabouts, in direct rebellion to a match that had been agreed upon in Shanghai before her birth. Her father had acted from honor—"Good faith," in his broken English. "Send my bones home, please, sir." Frank put a bullet in his skull, wrapped him in an old blanket reeking of opium and other filth, and dragged him over the nearest pier and into the greasy water in the harbor.

The local tong would go on looking for the white man in the pointed beard until the industry of the vigilance committee directed its efforts toward personal protection.

Frank made arrangements for the girl's burial in a Buddhist cemetery. During the religious ceremony, not a detail of which he followed, he thought of Evangeline Dierdorf.

"I didn't serve her well," he thought; "no, not at all." And began efforts to trace her movements from San Francisco.

In time, with help from the Pinkerton National Detective Agency until his capital ran out, he received a clipping from a newspaper in Carson City, Nevada:

> Responding to a complaint from an unruly house in this city Thursday last, police removed the remains of a young woman known only as Angie, dead of an abuse of tincture of opium; associates reported that she'd sought relief from pain owing to an extraction of eight badly impacted teeth, misjudging the dosage. She had been a resident of the house for some weeks. Burial has taken place in the cemetery for indigents.

Frank "sought relief" from a contraband bottle he'd held out from the general lot, and was ejected from his hotel for vandalism. A number of furnishings were smashed beyond repair, including a basin with a woman's eyelash stuck to it.

He found a billet not demonstrably different from the one he'd just left, submitted his resignation to the committee, and inquired at the Palace, as he'd done on and off throughout the autumn, about Abraham Cripplehorn. The clerk, a fair-haired consumptive from Wisconsin, sighed—Frank's was a familiar face across that marble-topped desk—and consulted his registration.

"Not checked in yet, sir; but he sent a wire reserving a suite. We expect him Monday next."

"Mr. Cripplehorn?"

The man signing the register, small in stature but well setup in a silk waistcoat, gabardine suit of clothes, high-heeled boots, and a Stetson that had never held a horse's fill of water, regarded him with one working eye; the other was store-bought, like Frank's ear. Frank, sensitive about that feature, knew when it was spotted.

"Would your name by chance be Farmer?" asked the man.

"It would, and not by chance. I'm told you know a fellow name of Locke."

Cripplehorn picked up his valise. "We'll talk in my suite."

There was a sitting room connected to the bedroom, with fresh flowers in a copper vase, deep leather chairs, and a Gainsborough print leaning out from a wall. Through a half-open door gleamed a brass bed piled high with pillows in tasseled shams. From inside his valise the guest of the hotel withdrew a matching leather case that opened to reveal three cut-glass decanters held in place with leather straps. Brass tags hung from tiny chains around their necks were engraved BOURBON, RYE, and BRANDY. Frank asked for rye and watched him unstop one of the decanters and pour golden liquid into a hotel glass. He paused two inches from the top.

"Shall I ring for ice?"

"I didn't come here to skate."

Cripplehorn smiled and filled the glass the rest of the way. He poured brandy into another.

They sat. Frank's host watched with amusement as he flipped half his drink down his throat. "You're the authentic article, that I can see."

"You're partial to that word. I read your book."

"I sometimes forget the literacy rate out here. I know the owner of a highly successful manufactory back East who can barely write his name."

"It's either learn to read or bonk yourself on the head with a rock from boredom. Things ain't as various out here as it says in your book. I'm a mite surprised I never heard of this Turnstile. I counted eighty-two dead by his hand."

"Eyewitnesses will embellish. His mistake was to go on killing after all his grievances were addressed. The good people of Virginia City broke him out of jail while he was awaiting trial for killing a popular bartender and hanged him off a railroad trestle. Three wives showed up to claim the body."

"I'd of kissed the ones with the rope for pulling me out of that." Frank put down the rest of his drink. "About Randy."

"About Randy indeed." Cripplehorn sipped brandy and set his glass on a low table between them. "He gave me a general delivery address in Wyoming, but all my letters came back for inability to deliver."

Frank stood. "I won't be taking any more of your time."

"I'd be grateful if you'd let me take some of yours."

"Who's asking, Cripplehorn or Dodger? I get jumpy

around fellows with more than one name. It's like carrying two sets of dice."

"The former. I find it easier to get around without dragging the burden of fame behind me. In certain places Jack Dodger is better known than Charles Dickens."

Frank didn't doubt that, not knowing who was this Dickens. He refilled his glass and sat back down.

Abraham Cripplehorn told him of his plan to charge admission to see Randy Locke and Frank Farmer settle their affairs in public.

"I don't see how far we'll get, seeing as how we'll all be in jail the minute what we're about gets around."

"I'm surprised you gentlemen are so concerned about the law, given your method of resolving your differences. However, dealing with such obstacles will be my contribution. I didn't just come up with this idea. I've had two years to think about it since I spoke with Locke."

"You talk a good game. What's the color of your money?"

From a pocket Cripplehorn produced a fold of banknotes in a spring clasp with an Indian head in copper and held it up. A fifty-dollar note was wrapped around the outside.

"I met a pump-organ drummer carried a roll like that in Rocky Fork. It was all singles inside."

"You're free to inspect it, once we come to an agreement."

"You seem mighty sure we will."

"Why would we not? Assuming you're still resolute."

"Don't you worry about that. What's to stop me from

crawfishing once I take your money? I don't need no business arrangement to put Randy in the ground."

"As I told Mr. Locke, the record of your association is fee simple that your word is good. This fifty is a deposit. The rest will go to the survivor of the contest—or his heirs should he expire shortly after his opponent."

"What if we go together?"

"That, sir, would be a windfall."

Frank unbuttoned his coat, exposing the Remington's cracked grip. "You never know in a crowd like that where a stray bullet may come from."

Cripplehorn smiled.

"I understand the implication, and I don't resent it. I will state that I am no gun man—you may inspect me if you wish, I go unarmed—and would be taking my life in my hands against either one of you. And to employ a surrogate would be to share the reward, which would render the exercise pointless."

"I can see you worked this out."

"It has been my ambition for some time now, as I said."

"I don't have heirs. You can keep my share if Randy gets lucky. I won't need it where I've gone."

"Then we have an understanding?"

"I reckon so. We been running around going on fifteen years, trying to kill each other for free. I don't see any sin in making a buck off it."

Cripplehorn freed the fifty-dollar note from the clasp, letting him see a second one underneath, and put the first on the low table. Frank scooped it up, stretched it between his hands, and held it up to the window. "I ain't seen one of these in so long we're plumb shy around each other." He folded it in quarters and poked it into his watch pocket.

The other man picked up his glass, sipped, and made a face as if it contained alkali water. "Unfortunately, the situation is the same as when I spoke to Mr. Locke, although this time around he's the one who can't be reached."

"He'll do the reaching, soon as he hears I'm in town."

"That's just what he said about you."

"And here I sit."

"Two years later. This time we'll accelerate the process."

ELEVEN

The press is an institution run by the inmates.

Major W. B. Updegraff (the W stood for Wisdom, but the men who accompanied him to sporting houses called him Dub) came out of Second Manassas with the rank of sergeant-major and a chunk of Yankee mortar in his right knee. He was Major to the staff of *The Barbary Spar*.

He hadn't set out to be a publisher. He won his first printing press, a lever-operated Columbian patented in 1813, playing poker in Tennessee. Before that he wasn't even a regular reader of newspapers, but it seemed everyone else was, especially the farther he moved West. The ten-cent price covered expenses, and advertising and jobbing (election leaflets, business cards, and letterheads) had kept his head above water during the Panic of '73.

He was forced to leave that first press in Yankton when a local manufacturer of fireworks came looking for him with a bullwhip. He bought another, a Prouty platen, when the Kansas Pacific Railroad left behind an end-of-track town in Colorado, cheap from a publisher who'd grown weary of transporting his equipment every time the railroad moved on. It now stood, an impressive arrangement of gears, rubber-covered rollers, and an enormous cast-iron flywheel with curved spokes, in a building constructed from packing cases within earshot of the splash whenever a drunk was robbed, slain, and flung into San Francisco Harbor. Its sign, printed in Olde English letters on a pine board, hung by chains from the spar of a ship that had run aground off Goat Rock, and for which the establishment was named.

The building was not much larger than a carriage house. This compact arrangement suited the Major, who in a trice could walk from the press to the lithograph stone with its polished slab of gunmetal-colored rock to the yellow-oak cabinet where lead type was stored in shallow drawers to his heaped rolltop desk with tubes of foolscap like piano-player rolls sticking out of the pigeonholes to the type-writer, a knee-high pile of ratchets, pulleys, and balance wheels mounted on casters with a treadle like a sewing machine, without overtaxing his bunged-up leg.

He never used the type-writer himself. He called it the Contraption, preferring to confine his mechanical acumen to the platen press. But every modern office had to have at least one type-writer on display, and he was loath to surrender any part of his tight quarters to anything purely decorative. He'd hired a male secretary away from a city superintendent to operate it, not to write copy but to bring an air of efficiency to his business correspondence. Young Greenfield took dictation as fast as the Major could give it—and he was a rapid speaker, brooking no interruption—and used all ten fingers on the keyboard; when the lad's pilot light was on, the noise sounded like an army of timberjacks clearing a stand of redwoods. On a truly productive day, the chopping of the strikers and the clunkety-clunk of the press producing sheet after sheet of dense print drowned out the foghorns bawling in the bay and the vibration shook dust and soot from the rafters.

The Barbary Spar advertised a circulation of twenty-five thousand. That figure was based on the calculation that at least five people were exposed to each issue of the biweekly journal. At that it was an exaggeration, because of the five thousand copies printed, five hundred were returned for credit by the merchants who stocked them.

Updegraff was built close to the ground and looked as if he'd shriveled inside his clothes: His open waistcoat, yellowed shirt, and trousers swaddled him, and in fact had the day he'd bought them. He was indifferent to male fashion and thought Greenfield a fop for blacking his shoes and changing his collar twice a week. He himself had worn the same green eyeshade since Dakota, cracked and spliced with sticking-plaster. The cigars that had burned holes in his shirt had left furrows on every surface in the office except the lithographic stone. The only thing he was vain about was his eyesight. The wire-rimmed spectacles he used for reading vanished into a clamshell case whenever someone approached. He was forty-two years old when Abraham Cripplehorn made his acquaintance, carrying a sheaf of neatly written notes on Palace Hotel stationery.

ILLUSTRIOUS GUN MAN STOPS HERE.

by Jack Dodger

Mr. Francis X. Farmer, known to readers throughout North America as the shootist ensnared in a "blood feud" with Mr. Randolph Locke, both originally of Texas, since the spring of 1868, is stopping in San Francisco and hopes that Mr. Locke will be doing the same when opportunity permits.

Asked the reason for the long enmity, Farmer said, "That's between Randy and me. I don't see how it's of concern to anyone else."

When this correspondent went on to inquire as to the character of his esteemed opponent, he replied, "He was one of the hardest-working hands who rode for the old Circle X, and what he lacks in skill with a carbine or rifle he more than makes up for with a hand iron. I carry around evidence of that, for anyone who doubts my word."

Farmer was alluding, in addition to two ancient scars on his chest and back, to the artificial ear of expert workmanship that substitutes for that appendage, which was shot off by Locke in Abilene, Kansas, in 1869.

Locke has not gone unscathed as a result of these associations. He lost much of the use of a leg when Farmer shot his horse from under him in Wyoming, ruining him for ranch work. He's said to have made his living since hunting wolves and buffalo and as a ranch cook. . . .

"No, I've not lost my taste for the affair," Farmer said when asked if time had cooled his ardor. "I don't reckon Randy has neither, and if he hasn't turned into a yellow skunk by now, I look forward to taking up where we left off in Salt Lake City."

Major Updegraff snatched off his spectacles and looked up from the sheaf in his hand. His visitor was a bland-enough-looking fellow despite his elaborate Wild West Show rig-out and false eye. He looked like a barbed-wire salesman who'd gotten too close to his samples.

"You're Dodger?"

"Professionally, yes. The name is Cripplehorn in private life."

"I've heard of this pair. For my money there's been too much romanticizing of this kind of range rat already. It drives away business and puts the vigilantes on the prod."

"If you're not interested—"

"I didn't say that. I'm just warming up for an editorial. My readers like it when I get my back up. You don't say where Farmer's staying."

"He asked me not to. He doesn't want reporters camping out in the lobby, like what happened with Locke when he was in town."

"That's all right with me. I can't get hotel advertising.

What brought you here? Why didn't you go to Gilbert at the *Examiner,* or Butler at the *Call,* or any one of a half-dozen others can buy the *Spar* out of petty cash?"

"They all wanted to turn it over to one of their own reporters, rewrite everything, and copyright it under the papers' names. I didn't write it for someone else's glory."

"Well, it could do with editing. You got three pages in the middle of midnight rides and bloody gun battles, with no one to attribute it all to. Were you there?"

"No, but it seemed kind of puny without it. I couldn't get Frank to say a derogatory thing about Randy till the end, and that was tame. The idea was to get him out here and lay the thing to rest."

"I can see where Butler wouldn't have any of it. His people are Quakers. Is it your intention to be there when it happens?"

"In a manner of speaking."

The Major lit his cold cigar, releasing a fresh shower of sparks onto his shirt and waistcoat. He brushed at them and squinted at the other through a screen of blue smoke. "You one of those jaspers likes to attend public train wrecks?"

"I'm an entrepreneur. I make my money off those same jaspers."

"I'm not one. I don't pay for outside copy, if that's what you're thinking. If I was to start doing that and my reporters found out, I'd have to pay them regular."

"I'm not. Are you interested or aren't you?"

"I ought to send a man to interview him himself."

"He won't get past the door. I've got Frank's word the story's mine."

"The word of a man-killer?"

"He's been called that and other things as well, but never a welsher."

Updegraff picked up a page. "Who's Mississippi Belle?"

"A boat I used to own. The story needed a woman."

The newspaperman drew a line with a soft black pencil and Belle was gone.

"How do I know you didn't make the whole thing up?"

"Isn't this the paper that printed the headline CUSTER'S VICTORY IN MONTANA?"

"That was the War Department's fault. They withheld the details so as not to spoil the Centennial celebration in Washington. I had to run a retraction. You don't develop a taste for crow, I can tell you."

"You can send a man with me to talk to Farmer. He'll convince him who he is quickly enough."

"Probably scare him out of town and leave me short-staffed." Updegraff's cigar had gone out again when the hot ash met saliva, but he didn't appear to notice. "Well, I can't use it as written, starting with the headline. I write those myself, and it has to fit the column. Most of the rest reads like a cheap novel. All this Buffalo Bill hogwash has to come out."

"That's acceptable, as long as you keep in the quotations and put my name on it."

"Don't you worry about that. One place you've got him

talking like Henry Ward Beecher and another like Davy Crockett. If I asked any of my people to claim credit, he'd up and quit."

"Will you send it out on the wire?"

"Oh, hell, yes. The eastern journals will be on this like buzzards on a dead elephant. I'm going to copyright it—don't get your bowels in an uproar, we'll share ownership—so they'll have to mention the *Spar.* I may have to increase my print run to what it says on the masthead."

TWELVE

Bad company is like a pox, and the unafflicted would be wise to avoid it.

The railroad man's name was Herbert, Henry Herbert. Right off Randy was disposed to dislike a man who hadn't a last name.

He was enormously fat—sideshow freak fat, the kind of fat that made a stranger turn to watch him, slack-jawed, as they passed on the street, like a runaway train on fire and passengers jumping off the vestibules to sure broken necks to get free. Globs of him pushed out under the hickory arms of his swivel chair, which groaned agonizingly like a cow breech-birthing, and if he had on a cravat—as seemed likely—you couldn't see it for the concertina folds of fat under his chin. Randy wondered why the man bothered. He was sweating in his office on the second story of a bank building in Phoenix, Arizona Territory, with the windows open creating a cross draft of pure furnace air, a slippery mess of overfed catfish who might just lubricate himself free of the chair if he weren't wedged in tight as a tick.

"I know your dealings with Frank Farmer," Herbert said. "To be honest, I'd rather be talking to him. This is more in his line of work, and I'm concerned about that leg."

"Just what *is* the job? The notice in the paper just said you wanted an unmarried man."

"A bit of drama, suggested by my partner; to get attention, he said. He was right. Since it ran I've turned away dozens of applicants. We're building a spur from Elgin to Calabesas in Pima County, a stone's throw from the Mexican border. We need someone to discourage the Apaches from endangering the workers."

"One?"

"I'd prefer a squad, but the treasury won't cover paying men just to stand around waiting to be needed. Some of the workers are experienced with weapons, so you won't exactly be alone. Of all who have come forward you're the most promising—if you're who you say you are—but, to be honest—"

His favorite phrase, it developed, like a profane man slinging around Jesus. "I don't shoot with my leg," Randy put in. "I'm best at close range, but I shot wolves and buffler from three hundred yards. I reckon I can scatter a batch of yammering savages on those scrub ponies they straddle down here."

The railroad man's chair groaned this way and that; thinking with his ass. Finally he swiveled to face his desk, dipped a pen in a squat bottle, scribbled something on rag paper with the name of the railroad printed across the top in bold letters with doodads on them, sprinkled sand from a pot on what he'd written, and blew away the loose grains. "Give this to Ralph Potter, the foreman. Go to Elgin and follow the tracks west. You'll need travel expenses."

A black iron safe with gilt lettering squatted in a corner. Grunting and blowing, the railroad man crab-walked his chair over to it on squealing casters, leaned forward, and worked the dial. He took a tin box from inside, opened it, counted out banknotes from a stack, put back the box, shut the safe, and gave the dial a spin. "One hundred dollars. That should cover the fare to Elgin—I'd give you a pass, but that stretch belongs to a competitor—provisions, and whatever other incidentals you'll need."

Randy took the sheaf of notes, stuck it in his worn cowhide poke, and put it in his hip pocket. The railroad man asked him if he wasn't going to count the notes.

"I reckon it's all there. You train men don't steal by the dollar. Anyway, I can always find my way back here."

It was March, although by the standards of most places it was July, especially the farther he went south across that parched territory, where through passengers got out at every poke-hole station to unstick their shirts from their backs and drink water from a pump. At every stop lay the same yellow dog in the shade of the station overhang, sprawled on its side as dead, the same plug-hatted Indian wrapped in a blanket sat with his back to the station wall, the same litter of scrawny boys wearing ropes for suspenders flocked around the alighting passengers looking to run an errand for a penny. Sixty miles of that, from Phoenix to Elgin, with nary a stick of wood in sight except what was required for support and couldn't be fashioned from the native mud like everything else. All the stations were made of it, frequently whitewashed although not always, with the red mud bleeding pink through the white.

Elgin was more of the same. The names of the businesses were generic: MERCANTILE, SALOON, LIVERY STABLE, BANK, as if the sheer dirt-pounding pressure of arid heat shriveled the imagination like the string of chili peppers hanging from every porch post, and painted directly on the dried mud. There was one mercantile, one livery, one bank, four saloons, with it seemed every horse in the vicinity tied up in front of the latter, heads hanging in the heat.

A fat blue fly landed on Randy's cheek while he was collecting his bedroll from the brass overhead rack, waited resignedly for him to swat it. When he didn't bother, it rubbed its front legs together, tested one wing, then the other, and lifted off, floating on the heavy air.

"You get used to it," said the old man in a split-bottom chair tipped back against the station wall, another fixture at every stop. "It's dry heat, not like Kansas or Missouri."

The newcomer finished mopping the back of his neck with a bandanna. "It's dry in a Dutch oven, but the biscuits burn just the same."

He entered the livery, where the cool dimness fell across him like mist. The attendant, a wiry sixty in filthy overalls, sat on an overturned bucket scooping sardines from a can into his mouth with his fingers.

"Buggy's hired," he said, eyeing Randy's game leg. "Expect it back at sundown."

"I need a saddle horse."

"You can have Patty. She's old but she's gentle."

"I said a horse, not a rocking chair. And a decent saddle, not one of them dishrags." A row of brittle-looking saddles drooped from a wooden rail, cinch straps stiff as straw. He'd sold his good one in Lincoln for the fare to Arizona Territory; he'd had his fill of cold and thought he might try his luck prospecting for silver in Tombstone or Bisbee. But the money ran out in Phoenix, just in time for him to see the notice in the *Herald*.

The livery man frowned, tossed the empty sardine can into a pile of manure, wiped his hands on his overalls, and got up to trot out a short-coupled sorrel mare with thick haunches. Randy looked at its teeth, felt its fetlocks, and inspected it for fistulas. "How much?"

"For the day or the week?"

"For the horse. I don't figure to be coming back here."

They traded, agreeing finally on thirty for the horse and ten for a McClellan saddle that looked as if it might last to Calabesas. Randy lashed his bedroll wrapped around the Ballard rifle behind the cantle and swung into leather, awkwardly on account of his leg but fast enough to satisfy the livery man he wouldn't fall off in town and bring shame to the enterprise.

Ralph Potter, the foreman, was a lean man in a leather waistcoat and whipcords, with stovepipe boots and a flat-brimmed, round-crowned hat like a town Indian's. He wore a self-cocker in a stiff cavalry holster on his hip. His pale blue eyes looked like steel shavings caught in cracks and he was burned deep cherry from sweatband to collar and from wrists to fingertips and likely was creamy white everywhere else, like an honest man. Randy figured he was honest enough, but disliked him on sight. He was inhospitable, but that was neither here nor there. There was something lacking in the man—not as obvious as a missing limb or a blind eye, but easy to spot just the same.

Decency, that's what was missing. Randy had seen it before, often enough to know better than to argue himself out of the suspicion.

"Goddamn it, I told 'em the Apaches are down in Chihuahua, holed up in caves avoiding General Crook. I'd sooner they sent a good working jack."

"Well, I'm here."

They had tents set up, the nearest shade being where they had come from and where they were headed, which was about the same distance. The graders were hauling their drags, the gandies dropping the rails into place with businesslike clanks and swinging their sledges, the Irish singing something from the old country, the Chinese working silently, no jabbering like their fellow expatriates who worked in town. A Negro boy in a flop hat and overalls carried around a bucket of water from which the Irish took a dipper and drank or sloshed it over their heads or both. The Chinese never sloshed, and some of them skipped their turns at a drink, seeming almost annoyed at the interruption to their labors. There was a covered chuck wagon and a dray loaded with barrels of water. Randy wondered what sort of man was in charge of the chuck.

Damn, now he was even *thinking* like a cookie.

Potter watched him watching the crew.

"The chinks are hard workers, and dependable as clap in Kansas City. They don't get drunk, don't fight among themselves, never go on strike, and stay away from whores."

"What about the Irish?"

"Ignorant as mules and twice as stubborn. Oh, they give you a week's work in a day, when they ain't hungover or beating each other's brains out or got a bee up their ass over some little thing. If I could breed 'em with the chinks, cross the micks' muscle with the yeller boys' sense of responsibility, I'd have this spur finished. The Irish are talking strike, just when I need 'em to work through Sundays before the monsoons shut us down for a month." The foreman shot a stream of tobacco, just missing the toe of Randy's boot; testing the distance, thought the other; between his indecency and Randy's patience. "Seeing's how you're here, you can draw your pay at the end of the week, then go wherever you like, so long as it ain't here."

"I was promised six weeks."

"Not by me, you wasn't. I can't stand to see a man drawing pay sitting in the shade. It gives the Irish ideas."

"What shade? That rake handle over there wouldn't keep the sweat off a sand flea. I didn't come all the way from Nebraska for no twenty dollars. I spent all the up-front money on trains and that fat town mare holding up a Yankee saddle."

"You got them, and you got to see some country. I was you I'd leave it at that." Potter laid a hand to rest on the handle of the self-cocking pistol.

Randy considered it; but he was saving that fight for someone else. "I'll draw that twenty now."

"At the end of the week, I said."

He pushed his hat back on his head, exposing pale skin from where it had rested to his thinning widow's peak. "Then I reckon I'll stretch out under the chuck wagon. Have somebody wake me it's supper, will you? Me, I'd pick one of the Chinese, but I don't like to tell a ramrod his business."

The foreman's left cheek caved in, getting the works between his teeth. Randy saw a couple of the Irish looking their way, getting ready to lean on the handles of their shovels. Finally he dropped his hand from his weapon and jerked his head toward the biggest of the tents.

The respective cool of the interior dried the sweat on the back of Randy's neck. There was a campaign table and chair, a leather-reinforced canvas bag like postmen carried tied in a Gordian knot by its handles to the center pole with a lock securing its flap, a cot, and a ledger the size of a plat book spread open on the table. It was where the foreman doled out the pay. He sat in the folding chair, hoisted a bottle from under the table, and slid it across the table. "No glasses. No fandango dancers neither. Just Old Pepper; and if the micks smell it out they'll beat each other to death trying to get it."

Randy made sure a nearby powder keg was empty and lowered himself onto it. "If you're looking to drink me under this table to avoid paying me, you better dig a hole." He uncorked the bottle, tipped it up, and let it gurgle.

"No. Hell, no. Out there I got to behave like it's coming out of my own poke, but to me it's just rebel scrip. I was to do the company out of a dime, they'd hunt me to China and take it out through my kidneys. I reckon you and I can reach an agreement."

"The Irish?" Randy wiped the back of his hand across his mouth and scooted the bottle back across the table.

"When the day's work's through and they ain't stripping the hide off each other's faces with their bare knuckles, they're talking strike. I can't take 'em all on, comes to that. But if an example can be made before they sort out their minds on the subject, I might could buy time, at least till the monsoons. By then we'll be so close to Calabesas I can finish with the chinks if I have to." He took a pull and pushed the bottle Randy's way.

Randy left it there. "I hired on to shoot injuns on the warpath. I won't murder a white man just to make a point."

"That's surprising talk, considering what I heard about you; but I'd never ask you to shoot an Irishman. They come in litters and we'd both be fighting 'em off the rest of our lives, which wouldn't be long."

"What, then?" But he was beginning to suspect.

Potter got up, went to the tent flap, and drew it aside. The view descended a slope to where a group of Chinese in flop hats and overalls were carrying twenty feet of iron rail.

"Take your pick," he said. "They're all of 'em alike."

Randy said nothing. The foreman looked back at him. "It'd convince the Irish we mean business. A chink today, maybe a mick tomorrow. It ain't as if the yeller boys ain't got a hundred cousins pouring in from Frisco every day."

Randy considered; then stood, scooped up the empty keg, and swung it at Potter's head. The staves collapsed like the sticks they were and one of the iron hoops lit on its side and rolled out the flap and down toward the latest patch of railroad, where it excited some interest, but only for a moment. Then the clank of the rails dropping into place and the clang of the sledges striking home the spikes resumed, echoing in Randy Locke's mind miles after it had faded from actual hearing.

In his poke he carried the six weeks' wages he'd hired

on for, freed from the bank bag with the aid of his old worn bowie and his own two hands, worn as well but still of service. Apprised of the atrocity by a wire from Ralph Potter, recuperating from a broken jaw in a mission hospital in Elgin, the railroad man in Phoenix posted a reward for his capture; as was typical of that industry, the amount settled upon was ten times more than had been lost.

Randy stopped for rest in a town that was so Mexican he suspected government surveyors of erring in drawing the line south rather than north of it. Every day seemed to be a cause for fiesta: the birth or death of an important saint, the anniversary of some skirmish between patriots and some tyrannical despot or other, thirteen whelps born to an old unparticular bitch thought barren, and she with teats enough to serve the bunch. All the signs were in Spanish and some bored woodcarver had hacked a monkey-faced Christ out of a saguaro cactus at the village entrance. The cantina where he found a room was run by a short broad Mexican with his hair cut in bangs and little triangular moustaches at the corners of his mouth. He put aside the Spanish-language newspaper he was reading to open the registration book. When he spun it his way to read the signature, his eyes stood out from his head.

"*Señor* Randy Locke?" said he. "*Randolph* Locke?"

"Not Randolph. Not to my face. Not in twenty-five years. *Por que?*" A man couldn't remain in Arizona long without picking up some of the lingo.

The little man spread the newspaper on the cracked piñon surface of the registration desk, pointing a ragged nail at an item in *El Noticias Telegrafo*. The first English word Randy spotted quickened his pulse: *Farmer*.

"How's your English?"

The little man glanced out the open front door, which looked out on the Rio Grande, brown and sluggish under the burden of violent history; Mexico three hundred yards away.

"*Señor*, I am not certain which language I am speaking now."

Randy stabbed a finger at the paper, cutting a cicatrix in the brittle newsprint with the nail. "Read it. In English." He stood a cartwheel dollar on its edge and spun it with a flick of the same finger. It made a white blur, mesmeric to the little man behind the desk, who snatched it up in mid-spin and turned the newspaper back his way.

"San Francisco, December eleventh," he read . . .

THIRTEEN

There is no better way of determining a friend's true character than to spend three days under the same roof.

San Francisco had lost nothing of its ability to separate a man from his capital; if anything, it had refined the process since Randy Locke's visit.

As damp, foggy winter melded into foggy, damp spring, the rates at the Palace had hollowed a deep gouge in Abraham Cripplehorn's Chautauqua earnings. Frank Farmer's more modest poke was reduced to the same state by the demands of the lesser hotels near the crumbling harbor. After some palaver, the two pooled their resources and went partners on a rented house occupied until recently by a shanghai agent known locally as Black Louie, and more recently still as a guest of the gallows. The walls were sufficient to hold up the roof, but held out neither noise nor drafts, and the roof itself had the unique property of releasing rusty water onto the tenants' heads even when the sun shone.

"How the devil is such a thing possible?" complained Cripplehorn, when a fresh gout teeming with iron particles and live wigglers suddenly seasoned his soup.

"A proper roof don't slant to the middle," Frank explained. "This one leaves pockets. Think of 'em as unplanned cisterns. If this was New Mexico, you'd be happy to have 'em."

"Well, it isn't, and I'm not. What's your reasoning on the rats? This morning I found a litter of them in my valise."

"Half this town's built of busted ships. I reckon the critters just come along with the timbers."

"What's keeping your friend? Updegraff says that piece went out on the wires two months ago. Maybe he's turned into that yellow skunk after all."

"I didn't say them words. That was pure Jack Dodger fiction, and if you remember right I was agin it. Randy's a lot of things, but he never tucked his tail 'twixt his legs and he ain't dumb enough to believe I ever said he did; not that it would keep him from coming here shanks mare if he had to. Either he's so far out in the high country he hasn't got the word or he's dead." Frank finished a game of Patience and peeled the dirty pasteboards off a dirtier oilcloth, one by one. "Either this table needs a new cover or I need a new deck. One more hand and I'll want a spatula."

Cripplehorn upended his last bottle of peach brandy into a tin cup that had come with the house. He ran a finger around the inside of the neck and sucked on it. "I entered this venture intending to clear enough to meet all the crown heads of Europe. Instead I'm incubating vermin and eating nail soup."

"Don't forget the baby meskeeters. A man needs meat."

"Do you really think he's dead?"

Frank shuffled the deck; or to be more precise, broke it free of itself from time to time like a batch of sliced bacon and rearranged the rashers.

"Nope. I know Randy better than anybody. He might let himself be swallowed up by a grizzly, if he got bored with the contest, but he'd come out that bear's ass with his Colt in his fist, asking after me."

"Can I quote you on that? It would read so well in *Harper's Weekly.*"

Frank pasted a jaded queen of hearts to the disreputable oilcloth. One of her eyes, thumb-smeared and stained with soot, appeared to be winking at him, with the tired automatism of an overqualified whore. "You come out here looking for color, you said. You wasn't specific as to the picture it got painted with."

Cripplehorn drained his cup, wobbled the last taste of civilization around inside his mouth, plucked his last cigar from his waistcoat, which needed mending at the seams, and lit it off the greasy flame from a coal-oil lamp that smoked like a rendering plant. Frank Farmer, he'd discovered, was less than the ideal roommate. He kept to his grooming, barbering his imperials, brushing his suit of unmatched pieces, and bathing when necessary, but as to the rest, living with him was like sharing quarters with one of those wild men one read about, raised by wolves. The outhouse was only ten paces from the back door, but when nature called, the nearest window would do: All the whitewash was eaten off the wall beneath every fenestration on the premises. He seemed to regard passing gas the supreme compliment to a meal well prepared (Cripplehorn considered himself a passably good cook, a condition forced upon him by self-sufficiency), scrubbed out his long-handles in the same sink where Cripplehorn washed his vegetables, and hung them from the same hook that supported the big frying pan in which most of their meals were prepared, dripping onto the iron stove and leaving circles of rust and essence of Frank Farmer on the surface.

It was about as far a cry from the crown heads of Europe as could be imagined.

Frank, in his turn, found Cripplehorn fell short of pards he'd lived with in past times. His coffee was so weak a fly could swim around on the surface, practicing its dog-crawl and floating on its back like some Oriental put'n'take, and it wouldn't wake a man up from a daydream. When the man retired, hanging up his clothes and fiddling with them so the pleats were just so, taking out his Dutch eye and polishing it with a little cloth and sinking it in a glass of water, he thought he might as well be living with a high-toned woman, only without the expected benefits.

The worst of it was that eye. On nights when the fog didn't stand between the house and the moon, a shaft passed through the window and lay on that glass. Ivory didn't sink, and so the eye floated on top, drifting this way and that, the way a real eye did in a human face, and lighting on Frank where he lay on his bunk. He couldn't shake the feeling that Cripplehorn was in charge of it and what it saw, and he couldn't sleep with a man staring at him wide awake from the bunk next to his.

This night he turned away from it onto his back. He stared up into the darkness beyond the red glow leaking from the poorly joined barrel stove and prayed to the Lord for Randy's safe conduct.

FOURTEEN

No man who has someone he can call upon for help is truly poor.

WANTED
Randolph Locke
is Sought for
Assault and Robbery
in Elgin, A.T.
A REWARD OF $1,000
is offered for information
leading to his arrest and conviction.

Randy spotted the shinplaster tacked to a corkboard in a combination general store and post office in San Diego. His description—height below average, thickset, full-faced—was right enough, but his own mother couldn't identify him by the pen-and-ink sketch that accompanied it. If he were the manhunting type he could keep pulling men off the street with vapid expressions and faces traced around the bottom of a whiskey bottle all day long and come away empty-handed. The storekeep, who was also postmaster, gave him not a second glance when he filled his order.

Not that being wanted signified anything. The more miles he put between himself and Arizona Territory, the less economically feasible it was for anyone to attempt to claim the thousand. He'd burned off most of the wages he'd had coming to him for refusing to shoot a Chinaman just getting that close to San Francisco and Frank. If he wanted to arrive with any stake at all he was looking at better than three hundred miles in a cattle car.

But worse was to come.

The guards aboard California trains had no regard for tramps. They made a thorough examination of the rolling stock before it moved, which meant jogging along and grabbing on outside the yards before the cars got to moving too fast. With his bedroll slung by a rope across his back, he missed on the first try and was falling behind when someone already aboard hung halfway out the open door of the car by the handle and stuck out a hand in a sooty fireman's glove. "Grab on, brother!"

Randy lunged for the hand, but he was at his limit, stumbled, and would have had to wait for the next train if another man aboard didn't take part. He got a grip on the edge of the door, linked hands with the first man, and hung on while the first man leaned out another six inches, grasped

Randy's outstretched hand, and with the added strength of his friend jerked Randy off the ground, through the door, and into a sliding skid across the straw-strewn floor that knocked the wind out of his lungs. He was still scratching for breath when the two men, aided by a third, robbed him of his bedroll, his Colt, and his poke, snatched him by his belt and the back of his collar, and slung him back out the door. He felt the first rib let go when he struck ground and lost count before he stopped rolling.

He was discovered by a kindly tramp who'd grown too old to ride the rods, scraping out a living picking up lost or discarded items along the cinderbed, fixing what could be fixed, and selling it in town. The old man loaded him aboard his wheelbarrow and delivered him to a free hospital run by a Mexican doctor who hadn't a license to practice in the United States. Felipe Guzman—"Doc Flip" to his white patients—stitched up his gashes, bound his rib cage with thirty yards of bandage, gave him a bottle of laudanum for the pain, and discharged him, apologizing that he couldn't spare the bed.

Standing on the boardwalk in front of the hospital, which still had part of a cow painted on its bricks from its butcher-shop origins, Randy went through all his pockets and came up with a dollar and change. He spent it in a Western Union office.

Abraham Cripplehorn went to the Palace Hotel on a daily basis, hoping for some word from Randy Locke. He was in the act of turning away from the marble-topped desk, having gotten the usual answer, when the clerk said, "Don't you also go by Dodger?"

STRANDED IN SAN DIEGO STOP NEED CASH TO GET TO FRISCO STOP WIRE GENERAL DELIVERY

R LOCKE

"It could be a scheme," Cripplchorn told Frank. "Somebody read my article and is using his name to raise easy money."

"It ain't." He was still looking at the yellow flimsy.

"What makes you so sure?"

"On account of I can't afford not to be."

"He does have fifty coming. Trouble is, I don't have it."

"How much you got?"

Cripplehorn opened his wallet, cordovan with gold corners, and got out two banknotes, a twenty and a five. A search of his pockets turned up a dollar in change. Frank found two limp singles and a cartwheel dollar.

"That should get him as far as Los Angeles."

"If he don't starve first. Hold on." Frank sat down on the wheezy old mattress, pulled off a boot, and went to work on the inside with his pocket knife. He came up with a twenty-dollar gold piece.

"Holding out on me?"

"I near forgot I had it. I had it stitched into the lining for when I tapped out again. It's from the fifty you gave me up front."

The entrepreneur took it and laid it on the tacky oilcloth with the rest. "I can get twenty for my watch; twenty-five if Goldfinch is in a good mood. He's my local bank when I need a stake."

"If I know Randy he'll need fresh duds. They're always last to go. He ain't the dress hoss I am."

"We don't make rent this month."

"If you ain't full of sheepdip, we'll be in the Palace before it's due."

The gunsmith in San Diego, a Swiss whose blond beard encircled his face like a wreath, handed the customer a Colt with most of the bluing gone. It was a .44 like the conversion he'd lost, only chambered for cartridges at the factory, and with a four-inch barrel.

"Got anything full-size?"

"That Smith and Wesson there on the wall."

"I mean a Colt."

"Just that custom piece in the case."

Randy looked at it through the glass. It had a stag handle and gold chasing on the nickel plate. The tag said fifty dollars.

"I'll get used to it." He turned from the counter, extending the short-barreled pistol from the shoulder, cocked it, and snapped the hammer on an empty chamber. "Trigger pull's tight."

"I can fix that. Dollar and a half extra."

He'd bought decent clothes and booked a day coach. He could just cover it and the purchase. "How soon?"

"Come back around three. I have two ahead of you." The gunsmith indicated a stockless Winchester in his vise and a Derringer in pieces on his bench.

Seeing the carbine gave Randy an idea. "Buy much off the street?"

"From time to time."

"Anybody come in trying to peddle a Ballard rifle?"

"Just yesterday. I turned him down. I didn't like his look."

"Leave his name?"

"No, but his kind generally hangs around the Sisters of Charity down on Ash."

"He didn't by any chance have a Colt to sell."

"No."

"How much to hang on to that short-barrel?"

"Five."

He put a banknote on the counter. "Hold off on that trigger till I get back."

He didn't entertain much hope. That train had been heading out of town. The bunch that jumped him wouldn't likely have circled back to turn his gear into cash. But men weren't as predictable as wolves and buffalo.

The neighborhood was worse than he'd seen in any dirty mining camp: lawyers with smut under their nails handing out cards on the corners, tramps sleeping in doorways, the kind of whore that was last to leave when a vein played out, ugly as half-broke sin. The buildings looked ready to fall down when a rat farted; they made a man want to walk down the middle of the street and take his chances with the drunken wagon drivers. He identified the Sisters of Charity by the line of unwashed men waiting for handouts.

One caught his eye, leaning without much hope against the iron railing of the front steps. Randy hadn't gotten a good enough look at those tramps to pick one out of a crowd, but this fellow was the only one carrying a bundle big enough to contain his Ballard. It was wrapped in an overcoat holier even than his clothes. He smelled of all kinds of human corruption, with an overlay of boiler soot, and someone had taken exception to his face sometime and tried to take it off with an axe or a big knife; the scar was old and puckered and ran from temple to chin. He had on dirty fireman's gloves, which rang a bell somewhere in the murk, but you couldn't kill a man just for what he wore on his hands.

Not with so many others present anyway.

Randy crossed the street to a boarded-up building and took a position in the doorway.

The line moved slowly, but in twenty minutes the man with the bundle was inside. Randy gave him twenty more to get to the front of the line, give Jesus His due, and eat his soup, then another twenty when that twenty ran out. His bad leg began to throb from all the standing; before long the pain would be fierce and constant.

But he forgot about it when the man came out and descended the stairs with a little more spring in his step than he'd had going in. Randy waited for him to hit the pavement, then crossed the street and fell in behind. They were two blocks from the charity house in a section empty of people when he quickened his pace and drew abreast.

"I'll have a look at that bundle."

The vagabond had better instincts than anticipated. Without pausing to look at the stranger he made a move for the inside of his torn overalls. Randy backed up a step, but he still had his bowie. The blade parted the man's shirtsleeve and carried away flesh from his elbow to his wrist. The bundle fell from under his arm, but Randy caught it and shoved the tramp the rest of the way off balance with his other hand.

There was something hard inside the holey overcoat. He grasped it, fingers closing around the familiar pistol-grip stock, and shook his rifle free. In the same motion he smashed the barrel across the man's face just as the man was scrambling to his feet, doubling the force of the collision. He went down hard on the ground, stunned.

Randy bent and searched his reeking clothes—not forgetting the pockets of the coat the tramp had used to swaddle the Ballard—but there was no sign of his Colt, just the clasp knife he'd intended to plunge into Randy. He threw it into a patch of weeds across the street.

He made a cane of the rifle, leaning on it to brace his bad leg, kicked the man in the side, snapping ribs, and went back to the gunsmith's shop for his new sidearm.

FIFTEEN

A man needs a close companion, if only to spare him from his baser instincts.

"Mr. Cripplehorn, may I expect payment this time in reasonably short order?"

The tailor, a tall Levantine with a scholar's stoop, wore the standard uniform of open-necked lawn shirt, striped trousers suspended by braces, and yellow tape measure around his neck. Pearl-headed pins glittered like captain's bars on his collar. He was on one knee beside the carpeted rise before the triptych mirrors, making chalk marks where the entrepreneur's uncut deckle-edged trouser leg crumpled at the instep.

The customer narrowed his working eye at his image in the basted-together morning coat; he prided himself on his ability to view himself with total objectivity. "Of course, my man. My allowance is due next week."

The tailor made a small adjustment in a measurement and recorded it in his little notebook, abandoning the discussion as pointless. With the forty-niners dying out and their grown sons making the Grand Tour to visit Italian statues and order suits in London, much of his business came from wayward progeny supported by payments from their respectable eastern parents to stay away. Since North America ran out at the Pacific, San Francisco was where they lighted. It was a generation that favored silk next to its skin and considered it bad form to settle a tailor's bill in less than a year. Meanwhile the Levantine's daughter wore hand-me-downs and his son was reduced to shaming his father in public wearing suits from Monkey Ward's.

His fitting completed, Cripplehorn resumed his last good suit and stepped out into a rare patch of Barbary Coast sunshine, absently groping for his silver-plated watch before he remembered. A glance at a tower clock told him he had an hour before the 3:45 got in: time enough to meet with his other partner.

"I was beginning to think you fell in the bay."

One glance at Frank Farmer said he was drunk and in a foul mood. The saloon, on Mission Street near the harbor, was a bare-bones affair aimed at mariners, with whitewashed walls naked but for a poorly wrought painting in a chipped gilt frame of a schooner caught in a storm at sea and shelves of whiskey cut with salt water from the Pacific, a beneficial combination, as it turned out: The liquor burned the throat, the brine cured it. Frank sat red-eyed at a corner table with a smeared glass in front of him and a nearly empty bottle at his elbow.

"Our arrangement was informal." Cripplehorn hung his Stetson on the hat tree and pulled out a chair. "If my session ran long, I would go straight to the station."

"I reckoned you'd growed dependent on that stem-winder and lost all track of time. In another fifteen I was fixing to meet the train myself."

Cripplehorn frowned.

"We agreed you're not to set eyes on each other until the contest. It's been years, and one or the other of you might lose sight of our objective in the heat of the moment."

"You saying I can't keep a hobble on myself?"

Not in your present condition. Aloud he said, "I'm less acquainted with Locke, based on our one conversation. We've a long way to go before the event. We need financial backing, and the legal matters will require money and time."

"Right now you can't raise the price of a drink even in this pisshole. What makes you think you'll find someone who can?"

"I've my eye on a young fellow I met at my tailor's. He's the man who gave me the idea to identify myself as the prodigal son of a wealthy and exasperated family, to forestall inconvenient questions about the condition of my finances: textiles, if I understood him correctly. He was in an inebriated state at the time, but he ordered three separate suits of evening wear and a half-dozen shirts made in Paris. He's a sporting man as well. I managed to separate him from ten dollars at euchre while we were waiting for a fitting. With a bit of finesse I hope to interest him in an investment that will grant him a measure of independence and a healthy return on our labors."

"Well, you just spent five times that ten in words. I lost a dollar to a man running a shell game in Denver during my Regulating time who I reckon swallowed the same dictionary."

"Then you see the value of my intentions."

"I knocked him flat and found the pea that belonged under one of them shells in his watch pocket. Being the nearest thing to law in that room I took back my dollar and fined him five more for being a tinhorn."

"You haven't met Sheridan Weber; of the Rhode Island Webers. He couldn't knock flat a blade of grass. Research the history of any one of these second-generation robber barons and you'll find his father strained him through a sheet."

"The cattlemen's association I worked for in Colorado was run by a fellow with consumption and a geezer couldn't hear a powder charge going off in the next room. You calculate this Sheridan wouldn't hire five men like me to take his investment out of your hide?"

"I think you should leave the business part to me and stick to your target practice."

"I'll take it up with Randy. He's a buffalo turd, but I'd rather sit downwind of him than listen to you gab about all the textile millionaires you met standing around in your long-handles."

Cripplehorn stretched himself, studying the men lined

up at the bar out of the corner of his eye. He felt inside a pocket, counting coins. He pushed out his chair and stood. "We're talking in circles. Why don't I get you something to soak up that skullbender and see if that bartender has a bottle of peach brandy he's keeping for medicinal purposes?"

"I ate yesterday. Just fetch me another one of these here, seeing's you're so good at euchre." Frank poured the rest of the whiskey into his glass.

A city policeman in his tight blue tunic and postman's cap stood with his foot on the green brass rail, drinking beer. As was the way of such establishments he had his end of the bar all to himself. Cripplehorn came up next to him and asked what varieties of liquor the bartender had on hand.

That individual stopped polishing a glass with a rag that left the glass in worse shape than when he'd started. He looked as if he'd stepped out of a sporting print, by way of too much butter and too many eggs. His nose was turned west ten degrees of his face and his apron hung straight down from his hard belly. "You got two choices, mister: bottle or glass."

"Glass. Not that one," he said, when the man set down the one he'd been working on and picked up a bottle. "One of those behind you." The pyramid of one-ounce glasses standing on the shelf looked as if he'd started them earlier in the rag's ruination.

"Ten cents."

He pushed a dime across a resistance of spilled whiskey

turned into mud from the grit on the bar and leaned in close to the policeman, who was staring into his beer and chuckling quietly at the exchange. Lowering his voice to a murmur, Cripplehorn said, "Officer, do you see that fellow sitting at the corner table?"

"I saw him. I don't miss much. This is my first drink today." He might have brought his brogue straight off the boat.

"What do the local statutes say about carrying firearms in the city?"

"They're to be checked at the station upon arrival and picked up upon departure, on pain of fine or incarceration." He appeared to have memorized the official language. "It's a peaceful place, mister, mostly. Anything you heard about road agents and vigilantes is way out of date. We confine all that truck west of Montgomery Street, where we know where to find the bad element when required." A pair of gray eyes set in a young hard face with black sidewhiskers took in the man making the inquiry. "What's your interest? You look like a hideout man to me."

Cripplehorn smuggled a look over his shoulder. Frank sat with his hands wrapped around his glass and his face almost touching it, his hat entirely obscuring his features. The entrepreneur knew the danger posed by men who appeared to be in torpor. But he wasn't looking in the direction of the bar.

Carefully, Cripplehorn unbuttoned his coat and spread the tails for the officer's inspection. "I don't have use for percussion weapons. The knife is for my personal protection."

"The ordinance don't say nothing about knives, so long as they ain't put to use. I'm waiting for an answer." He was standing straight facing Cripplehorn, his beer forgotten.

"I suspect that man I pointed out of wearing a pistol under his coat."

"Ain't he your friend?"

"It's for his own protection I'm asking. If he could be placed in a cell until he's sober, you'll find him a model citizen upon release."

"Gus, see to them at the other end."

The bartender had moved to within earshot of the low conversation. He nodded and carried the bottle to where a group of men dressed like teamsters was staring at the schooner in the painting waiting for it to sink.

"You see the pistol?" asked the man in uniform.

"No, but I can't imagine him without one."

"What's his name?"

"Frank Farmer."

The stiff-visored cap moved back, propelled by the muscles in the officer's forehead. "The gun man?"

"Retired."

"I never heard of such a thing happening this side of a churchyard."

"He's not wanted anywhere, if that's your concern."

"Farmer, huh?" He tugged at his sidewhiskers. Cripplehorn could read the man as easily as an amateur card player:

No one wanted to be a street patrolman forever. Finally the officer threw a coin on the bar.

"Keep him here if you can. I might need help."

"Try not to hurt him. He's a white fellow when he isn't in his cups."

SIXTEEN

Partnerships are based on personal regard and mutual trust. Where one is missing, the other is inconsequential.

He spotted Cripplehorn's exaggerated hat before the train rolled to a stop. Alighting, he avoided shaking hands by carrying his bedroll by its strap with one hand and his Ballard with the other. "Where's Frank?"

"He's arranged accommodations. Have you?"

"I ain't got the price. I'll camp outside town. I sure do hope you wasn't lying in that newspaper story."

"There's no need to worry about that."

"I like to worry, Dodger. It's got me this far."

"It looks like you took the rocky road."

"I ran into some excitement, but I'll heal. I won't ask you again about Frank."

"You'll have to accept my word he's in town. I can't take the chance of old associations come to grief before their time."

"That's a fancy way of saying I can't keep a fence on my own self."

"I never doubted it, but I'm not so sure about Mr. Farmer."

"You like to light both ends of the match, Cripplehorn."

"I'd consider it a favor if you'd call me either Cripplehorn or Dodger; not both. I'm told the vigilantes are inactive at present, but aliases have a way of exciting old passions. Are you hungry?"

"I could eat the stink out of a skunk."

Randy checked his gear in the station. They went into the Harvey House, where a hostess in a crisp white apron offered to help Randy into an alpaca coat from a rack.

"No thanks. I ain't cold."

Cripplehorn said, "It's a house rule. They won't seat you otherwise."

"What else do I need, a plug hat and a monkey stick?"

"Just a coat."

He thrust an arm into a sleeve. "Place sure has got toney since I was here last. Next time I'll have to bring along a brass band."

"I think you'll find the food's worth it."

"I won't appreciate it. I been eating my own cooking so long I can't tell a potato from buffler hump."

They were seated in a clean bright room with checked tablecloths. Another young white-aproned woman took their orders and moments later set roast sirloin and boiled sweet potatoes in front of Randy and a pile of blue-point oysters before Cripplehorn. Everything was on Santa Fe

Railroad china. Randy watched his host pick up a half-shell and slide an oyster into his mouth. Cripplehorn noticed him staring and raised his brows.

The other shook his head. "Just curious to see if you bothered to swallow."

"They're a fine source of iron."

"You can get that sucking on a horseshoe nail." He cut off a piece of steak. "This is a fair spread. You must be in tall cotton."

"The meals here are seventy-five cents apiece."

"Six bits, that's what I'm worth to you?"

"A moment ago you thought it was two dollars. It's still the same steak, is it not?"

"It should be, but it ain't. Cow lives its life, maybe she knows she'll wind up on a plate somewheres, ask her does she want to go for a banknote or pocket jingle? I reckon it's all in the way you look at it, providing you're a cow and got no vote in the election."

"Is it necessary always to be colorful? It must be a constant drain on the imagination coming up with all these frontier aphorisms."

Randy chewed his steak, letting the juice slide down his tongue. "Finding the time ain't much of a challenge. To read your books, a man'd think there wasn't time to use the outhouse for all the gunnies and greedy bankers and injuns on the warpath slinging lead like it grows on trees. I counted eighty-seven rounds from a six-shooter in that Brimstone Bob thing."

"I've never pretended to a knowledge of firearms. Blame my editors."

"It don't signify: I'm talking about the life. I never read a word about all the time spent pushing the same two dollars around a card game in some line shack watching the snow pile up or sitting around some shit town playing mumblety-peg from noon till sundown waiting for the two-fifteen to get in from Cheyenne. I spent a year in Bismarck betting on when a busted gate would fall off its hinges. I reckon some of the boys are still there waiting."

"There's such a thing as literary license."

"It needs renewing."

Cripplehorn slid another oyster down his throat and chased it with coffee. "I'm sure the world is holding its breath until you publish a novel of your own, with all the slow time put in. Against my advice, Pat Garrett insisted on putting that same lethargy into his life of Billy the Kid. *Petticoat Betsy, the Bandit Princess,* with all its relentless action and dearth of introspection, outsold it a hundred to one."

Randy swirled a piece of steak in its juice, watching the fat coagulate.

"You know something?" he said. "I don't believe you ever met Garrett. I'm starting to believe the closest you ever got to a Jack Dodger book is them copies you sling around like grain seed. Fact is, Mr. Cripplehorn, I don't think you ever done a thing in your life a man could brag on. You're so full of compost I'm surprised you don't grow beans out your ears."

"I won't argue the point or we'd be here all day. Past performance doesn't guarantee future results, as they say in New York City. You know as well as I that what's between you and Farmer is mother's milk back East. People are plunking down their hard-earned dollars from Philadelphia to St. Louis just to see Buffalo Bill and his red-eye-swilling cronies pretend to shoot each other with cap guns onstage. They'll tire of that soon enough and start demanding the real thing. I have ancient Rome as an example to back that up. Those old emperors filled arenas larger than Madison Square Garden to see Christians try their luck against African lions; knowing all the time how the contests would finish. I'm—we're—going them one better. No one can say who will come out standing from a blood duel between Randy Locke and Frank Farmer."

Randy scooped a forkful of sweet potatoes dripping with butter into his mouth and followed it down with a pull from the pint of Old Pepper he'd bought in San Diego.

"Well, I thank you for the top billing." He grinned at Cripplehorn's sudden interest. "Didn't think I knew about such things, did you? It so happens I'm a reading man. When I plunk down a dime for a newspaper I get all the good out of it, from President Garfield getting shot to who's playing the Bird Cage in Tombstone. But I know who'll come out standing. Frank's an artist with a Winchester, but if I was a fair man I'd give him a second's head start when it comes to hip guns. Not that I would," he added, chewing steak. "You don't ever give the other fellow a break when it comes to killing, like in them books you claim you wrote."

"I know an alienist in Chicago who'd pay to cut up your brain and see what's inside," Cripplehorn said; "but I have my standards. I want you to sign this." He drew a folded sheet of rag paper from his inside breast pocket and pushed it across the tablecloth.

"What is it?" Randy left it where it was.

"Look it over. It's not a rattlesnake."

He wiped his hands on his shirt, picked up the paper, and snapped it open, holding it out at arm's length until the type-written letters arranged themselves into language. His lips moved as he read.

"What is it?" He put it down.

"Merely a letter of agreement, attesting to the terms we've discussed: an equal division of the proceeds from your competition with Mr. Locke, between myself and the survivor, or his designated heirs should he encounter a fatal wound as a result. You can read, can't you?"

"I told you I read newspapers. I stuck through fourth grade like everyone else. Did Frank sign this?"

"He's considering it, as would any man of foresight. You may take as much time as you like, and consult an attorney if you want. There's nothing in it we haven't spoken about already."

Randy refolded the paper and pushed it back.

"I'll sign it when Frank does."

Cripplehorn twisted his face into something he hoped was ironic.

"He said the same about you. Are you sure you haven't been in contact with him since Salt Lake City?"

"If I was he'd be dead; or *I* would, if he catches luck. But we both worked for the old Circle X, and there was never nothing between the outfit and its hands but a handshake."

"That was then. Times have changed. You can't put a handshake in a safe."

"A paper can burn up. A handshake never does. Some things don't ever change."

"But there must be a record!"

"What's that, when one or both of us is in the ground? You city folk put too much store in records and such. They won't grow flowers on any of our graves. I won't sign it, and neither will Frank. I reckon I know him that well, if nobody else does."

Cripplehorn picked up an oyster; put it back. He wiped his hands on his napkin. "I'll never understand your type."

"That's the difference between us, Mr. Cripplehorn—or Mr. Dodger, whichever it is—Frank and me, we understand your type right down to the ground."

"A handshake it is, then; against my better judgment." He stuck his hand across the table.

Randy took it, in a grip that brought water even to Cripplehorn's false eye. When the entrepreneur tried to pull himself free, Randy increased the grasp. An iron tooth showed in a bunkhouse grin.

"You know why us frontier types put so much store in this here ritual?"

Cripplehorn shook his head; at a loss between freeing his phalanges from their punishment and Randy Locke's use of the term *ritual.*

"On account of if you don't hold up to it, the next time we show our hands is around the handle of a six-shooter. That's what this western hospitality you're always hearing about has to do with. If you don't prove yourself to be a gentleman, you gave up your right to be treated gentle."

He let go then, and mixed a forkful of rare sirloin with sweet potatoes. His face registered full approval of the flavor.

"I don't know why a man'd drop two bucks in New York City on six bits' worth of grub like this in Frisco," he said. "I reckon that's the difference between a railroad baron and a man works for plain wages."

Abraham Cripplehorn kneaded feeling back into his fingers and wondered for the first time if his wits and a belt knife were sufficient for survival in the American West.

SEVENTEEN

Diplomacy is crucial to enterprise.
Many a promising arrangement has failed for lack of a judicious word.

"One watch, tin," said the clerk behind the bars.

Frank said, "Platinum, you ignorant son of a bitch."

"One wallet, empty."

"I had a dollar in it when I got here."

"Take it up with the day man."

"Forget it. I'd as lief start over clean anyway."

"One Remington Frontier Model revolver, forty-five caliber. You need to replace those grips."

"I'm used to 'em."

"One cartridge belt and holster, cowhide."

He strapped on the belt and slid the weapon into the worn wraparound holster.

"One quarter, two nickels, one penny: thirty-six cents total. Sign here."

Frank Farmer scribbled his name on the receipt the clerk

had thrust through the opening in the bars and left the jail. No one was waiting for him outside the ironbound oak door leading to a back street. His clothes were rumpled, his imperial whiskers blurred with stubble, and one eye was nearly swollen shut, although he allowed as he'd given as good as he got when the men in uniform dragged him out of the saloon; one had gone over the bar into the bottles in back, he'd elbowed another's nose flat, and the drunk-and-disorderly they'd dumped into the neighboring cell the next day said he'd heard a third man wound up with a splint on his arm.

A judge with hair sprouting from his ears had sentenced Frank to three days underground for concealing a firearm and tacked on another ten for resisting arrest. He'd been given the choice of paying a fine of fifty dollars instead, but being as how he'd had only a dollar thirty-six cents to his name it wasn't a choice at all.

A wooden barber pole scratched all over by men striking matches hung outside a brick building on the corner. He turned in through the door. "Shave."

A man in striped shirtsleeves with his hair parted in the middle looked up from the newspaper he was reading in a chrome-and-leather chair and took him in from head to foot.

"Fifteen cents."

Frank slapped a quarter on the counter, stirring loose hairs there. The barber got up, made change from a General Jackson cigar box, and snapped the creases out of a cotton sheet.

The shop was all white enamel and black-and-white tile, with oak cabinets containing personalized shaving mugs and foo-foo juice in ornate bottles with glass stoppers. It smelled of citrus. Advertisements on the walls illustrated various sports with splendid curls and elegantly curved moustaches, and signs assured customers YES, WE CUT WET HAIR and offered special rates for children under age ten. Men wearing tights struck pugilistic poses inside pasteboard frames—showing off, thought Frank, for the lady in her underwear in the middle.

Reclined looking up at the pressed tin ceiling, he eased the Remington out of its holster and rested it on his lap under the sheet.

The barber whipped up a lather in a mug with a badger brush. "Interest you in your own mug? Fifty cents. Your name on it in copperplate, script, or fancy old English."

"What's wrong with the one you're using?"

"Nothing, only it's common. Folks come in, see your name there in the rack, they know you're quality. I could stand here all day and tell you the business deals got made right here on the premises."

"I'm certain of that, this place being so close to the jail. Slap on the soap and don't mess with my beard and moustache. I do my own trimming."

The razor's gentle scraping lulled him into a half-doze. When the street door opened, tinkling the copper bell mounted on it, he came awake and tightened his grip on his revolver.

Abraham Cripplehorn glanced around the room and smiled when he saw Frank. He was panting a little.

"You're next, mister," said the barber. "Today's newspapers there in the basket."

Cripplehorn nodded, but his eyes remained on the customer. "I took a chance you were here when I missed you at the jail. They let you go early."

"I got ten minutes off for good behavior. You got ten seconds to talk me out of drilling you where you stand." He lifted the Remington, making a bump in the sheet.

Cripplehorn riffled a pad of banknotes. "Barber, give this man your best shampoo and haircut."

The bump flattened.

It came about this way:

After seeing Randy off on a cable car to the Oakland side of the bay, Cripplehorn called upon Sheridan Weber in his permanent suite at the Eldorado. French doors opened on a balcony overlooking most of the city, and his family crest, griffin rampant on a field of flax—aged artificially to disguise Weber *pere*'s recent purchase—hung above the four-poster. Cripplehorn held the door for a waiter pushing out a butler's caddy heaped with silver-covered dishes.

Young Weber stood in the middle of the Oriental rug in his underwear, curling a pair of black dumbbells. The exercise appeared to have made no difference in his hollow chest and slight paunch. His red hair was arranged in ringlets to disguise encroaching baldness and his attempt at recreating his father's rich muttonchop whiskers had so far been no more successful than his fitness programme. He wore a monocle, of all things. His visitor thought the real Jack Dodger, whoever he was, would blush to write such a character into one of his books.

"'Morning, Abe!" Weber strove to be as democratic as his sire was autocratic. "You're up and about early."

"It's five P.M., Sherry. The nighthawking life has thrown your internal clock off the rails."

"Ah, well. Sundowns are as pretty as sunrises, I'm told; and one is awake to appreciate them. What have you there, the opening of another blood-and-thunder novel? I can't keep up. I'm still slogging through Brimstone Bob."

"This won't take long. It's only two pages, and the wording is the same on both." He thumbed the sheets in his hand to demonstrate their brevity.

"Your last will and testament? Am I to witness the division of your worldly acquisitions?"

"That would be even briefer."

Weber tossed his dumbbells onto the bed, mopped his face on the towel draped around his neck, and took the sheets. From the lines of concentration on his forehead his visitor realized he was one of those men who had difficulty reading when someone was watching them. Cripplehorn strolled out onto the balcony, gazing out over the city spreading out from Telegraph Hill and across the bay; from his perspective, a handspan alone separated Frank Farmer from Randy Locke. He'd felt far more at ease when half a continent stood between them.

"Excellent!" said Weber, when he came back inside. "I'd thought these frontier types never put their names to anything."

"It took some convincing." Cripplehorn privately prided himself upon his ability to make two signatures appear as if they'd been written by different hands; he'd even thought to use two different colors of ink. He was grateful that actual specimens of the men's script were unavailable for comparison. "What about your end?"

"What sort of expenses are we talking about?

"A thousand, to start."

"Indeed, that much?"

"The situation is unique. On top of printing, advertising, travel, and accommodations, we're bound to encounter resistance from the authorities."

Weber returned the contracts and took a shirt off a hanger in the wardrobe. "My father is always entertaining public servants in Providence. My observation is they're sporting men."

"Many of them are, but they answer to the public. Wives in particular are opposed to exhibitions involving violence. You can't stage a legal cockfight in Texas, whose state bird ought to be the one-eyed rooster. In Washington there's a move afoot to outlaw prizefighting anywhere in the country. You can imagine the hue and cry when we propose a duel to the death."

"Women can't vote."

"Their husbands can. You'd be surprised to know how much influence a domestic arrangement can exercise in the privacy of a polling booth."

"You propose to bribe the authorities?"

"A man who can be bribed is a man who can double-cross you. He must be bought."

"And you think we can do this with a thousand dollars."

"I'll do the horse-trading. That's my end."

Weber stepped into a pair of checked trousers, tucked in his shirttail, and pulled braces over his shoulders, observing the effect in the full-length mirror on the wardrobe. "Just how much do I stand to clear from this arrangement? After all's said and done, it doesn't seem as if it will be enough to earn independence from my father."

"Mr. Weber, I think you want his approval more than anything else; to prove to him that you, too, can be a self-made man. The fact that the opportunities aren't as plentiful as they were in his time enhances the success. In addition to attendance fees, I intend to charge newspapers and magazines for interviews with my clients and will offer an exclusive with the survivor—if there is one—at auction before the event. I have contacts—subscriptions, anyway—with several of the major eastern newspapers, as well as *Harper's Weekly, Frank Leslie's Illustrated Newspaper,* and *Ned Buntline's Own,* and expect to hear from others once the news gets out. I estimate our enterprise will clear at least a hundred thousand once all the dust has settled." He twisted his face into a mask of concern. "I must warn you that there will be an inconvenience."

The young man—he was thirty, but a chronic adolescent—paused in the midst of tying his cravat. He watched Cripplehorn's worried reflection in the mirror.

"I know you're a modest man, Mr. Weber, who would go to any length to avoid sensation. That may not be possible in this case. I'm very much afraid that the journals will attempt to portray you as the greatest promoter of entertainment since P. T. Barnum. Your likeness will appear in the vulgar press, your every movement recorded: the entertainment venues you visit, the men and women who accompany you. Reporters will gather around you wherever you go. Your opinion will be sought on every subject. I'll understand completely if in the light of this intelligence you decide to abandon our business arrangement and avoid the nuisance."

There was always risk involved; a man pushed his chips into the center of the table and fought the urge to hesitate before taking away his hand. It was like standing on a bridge railing and looking down into a creek that didn't appear nearly as deep as it had before he'd accepted the boyhood dare to jump. A rocky bed and a fragile tailbone spelt disaster. Sometimes he wondered if that wasn't why he lived the way he did, for that heart-stopping moment when fate could go either way, and that the money was just another way of preserving it in a scrapbook. It was a test of courage, and it made a man understand what drove a Randy Locke and a Frank Farmer.

The time for the shakes and self-recrimination would come later, after the moment passed. And then he would plan his next.

The moment this time was briefer than usual. He saw the light of glory in Sheridan Weber's dull eyes.

"Barnum, you say?" He resumed dressing. "Coarse bounder. They say he lived openly with Jenny Lind."

"They say a great many things. It's all very vulgar, and so—public." Cripplehorn almost shuddered, then thought better of it. A man could go too far even with the idiot son of a pompous ass.

"Indeed. But I suppose one must take the lemon along with the sugar."

"You're most unselfish. Now, I may be able to keep your name out of it. Mind you, these journalists are tenacious, and can be thoroughly unscrupulous. I can't promise to be successful, and I wouldn't want to influence you with false—"

"That would be an expenditure of effort far beyond its worth. There's too much else to be done if this venture is to succeed." He shrugged into a Prince Albert coat cut for a younger man, put on a gray bowler, and selected a gold-knobbed stick from an assortment in a hollowed-out elephant's foot beside the door. "The money's downstairs in the safe." He reached for the knob.

Cripplehorn beat him to it. "Allow me."

EIGHTEEN

The human element is the open question in any transaction; one cannot allow for it, only prepare for difficulties.

I'm back; did you forget me?

No reason you shouldn't. My life would make a diverting book, but not as fast reading as Mr. Locke's or Mr. Farmer's. I wouldn't be its hero, only its narrator.

I'm the fellow who brought this whole affair to your attention, back when the West wasn't anyone's never-mind but the two men at the center. I reckon I should have took out the copyright when I had the chance.

Apart from a couple of wranglers working the Wild West crew, I'd had no contact with any of my fellow Circle X hands in sixteen years, and nearer seventeen. They didn't remember me, for which I was grateful, given the extent of my contribution to the outfit.

That season I'd helped birth a foal—getting in the way

mostly, ranch work and me being casual acquaintances at best. It's a wonder that critter isn't still in there.

I think of that colt from time to time: scrawny thing, more leg than anything else, and not sure what to do with them except try to stand, and for the first half-hour or so he found that challenge enough, doing splits like an acrobatic dancer I paid a nickel to see in a shack in Dry Fork they called the Opera House. He's dead now, most likely, or worse, tied up to some damn tinker's wagon, hanging his head and waiting to be rendered down for glue to stick a heel on some lady's pumps. I hadn't any contact with Randy or Frank in all that time, but I sure knew what they was about.

The Buffalo Bill outfit was touring Europe. For those of us in the press corps—what manager Nate Salsbury called it, after the crew in Washington that was writing down everything President Arthur had to say, which for pure interest wouldn't fill anyone's idea of a book worth peddling—the time dragged. A man got his fill of empty palaces, fallen-down temples, and busted statues in museums, and after a while even the spectacle of plains Indians chasing pigeons around St. Mark's Square for supper lost its charm. What time I didn't spend embroidering on Cody's career for press releases and souvenir pamphlets I whiled away reading newspapers, for whom Farmer and Locke never seemed to lose appeal. They came in bundles by ship from the States; but even the journals in London and Paris and Rome picked up items of general interest by way of the Trans-Atlantic cable. I still have cuttings in which *Monsieur* Locke and *Signor* Farmer are prominent. I can't read them myself. How those old emperors and popes managed to take over so much of history talking gibberish is beyond me.

See, nothing much of real interest had happened in the creaky Old World since *Herr* Bismarck whupped Louis Napoleon more than ten years ago, and what with "Bison William" and Annie Oakley and their passel of red Indians splashed across posters on every vertical surface from Buckingham Palace to the Parthenon, it seemed Europeans couldn't get enough of scalpings and gunfights and other colonial truck; it reminded them of Guy Fawkes and other excitements they'd got too civilized to let happen again, and missed, for all the pettifogging in Parliament and the Hague. Scuttlebutt said Salsbury approached Cody with the idea of inviting Frank and Randy to join the excursion, but Cody was agin it; seems he'd had his fill of taming such folk after Wild Bill Hickok shot out an acetylene spotlight from a Chicago stage because it hurt his eyes, showering sparks over the paying customers.

I was sorry to hear it. I'd grown weary of injecting nonexistent Indian battles and physically impossible feats of marksmanship into the official record, and could have done with some unadorned anecdotes from the Genuine Article. So I took my excitement from pallid, third-person accounts of that contest that had been going on since before the smoke had cleared from the War of the Rebellion.

That pair was about as hard to track as a grizzly through dry cornstalks. They left their sign on every scrap of newsprint those tramp steamers could carry without sinking. I reckon them that sank, when they're discovered and raised, will be found to have ferried their share, all clumped together like Spanish coin. Frank and Randy would shake their heads at the places their names had gone where they never did; some places they probably never heard of.

I knew about Abilene and Salt Lake City, though I craved for details I wouldn't know for many years, when I was able to collect them from what the legitimate historians call "primary sources." When all the pomp connected with placing the whole business before a paying audience came about, I learned the name Abraham Cripplehorn (and made up my mind about that fellow's character based just on the scanty evidence presented between the lines; I was on a personal basis with Ned Buntline, that unprincipled sot, and had built my opinions on that model). I followed his efforts to settle their differences—for the price of a ticket—before the court of public opinion, and thought about it long and hard when my company visited the Coliseum, hoping to stage the exhibition on the site where all those gladiators had made their last bloody stand. Nothing had changed exccpt the tin hats.

And I read about that business in San Francisco, where the impetuous behavior of the principals nearly brought it to an abrupt end.

A fellow had to travel a fair piece from the city of Oakland—and on foot to boot—to find a place to set up camp. The whole state was settled worse than Ohio. Randy had begun to think he'd have to walk clear to Nevada for unclaimed country when he found a grown-over vineyard with a weathered house and barn leaning towards each other like a couple of drunks looking for support and a sign in front where a bank had slapped its brand. He busted up the sign for firewood and after he'd cooked and eaten some beans and bacon and drunk coffee he found a cozy spot inside the barn among some old straw. The barn looked as if it would fall down about the same time as the house, but he had a cowboy's superstition about empty houses and ghosts: No one ever heard of a haunted barn. He lay on his back on his blanket, watching blue twilight steal in through the loft, and shot the first bat that showed itself, for the practice. The odor of sulfur and cordite lingered and lulled him towards sleep. A night like that made a man feel in harmony with existence. When the thing was done and Frank was in the ground, he reckoned he'd spend his cut on a grand house on top of some mountain and camp out in the backyard every night.

In the morning he walked a mile into the town the bank belonged to, all brick with a school and a library and even a Catholic church, and sent a wire to Cripplehorn letting him know where he could be found. He asked the clerk for the location of the livery.

"There isn't one."

"What kind of town don't have a livery?"

"Our kind. Most folks have their own horses. We're carriage trade here. I can't remember the last time I saw a man sitting smack-dab on top of a horse." His eyes flicked over Randy's range gear.

"Well, what do you do when you need a carriage pulled?"

"You might ask Lyle Miller if he's got a horse to spare."

"Where's his spread?"

"He's not a rancher. He owns the local milk route."

He got directions to a windowless building with wide double doors at the top of a wooden ramp. A sign reading SIERRA FARMS FINE DAIRY PRODUCTS ran across the front.

The doors were spread open. Randy climbed up the ramp into a place that smelled like a well-kept stable. Horses occupied ten stalls and five wooden milk wagons stood in a neat row along the back wall with the company's name painted on their sides. Tall milk cans gleamed spotlessly in a ten-tiered wooden rack erected across from the horses. In a little office built from two partitions in a corner, a squint-eyed old runt wearing a white shirt and necktie tucked inside clean overalls and a by-God Panama hat looked up from a ledger on a tall desk that was designed for standing behind, grinned, and said, "Howdy, cowboy. What can I do you for?"

"You Miller?"

"I favor Lyle. Miller's my father. Yep, he's still alive. Ninety-eight last month."

"Maybe he's dead and you just didn't notice. Where's the farm, Lyle?"

"Oh, the name? That's just for the customers. No one wants to buy milk from a factory. I get my stock from all over the county, depending on who's selling it cheap. You looking for a job delivering? You don't look like much of a milk drinker to me." His merry old eyes took in the rifle and belt gun all over again fresh. He chuckled.

"I'm through having anything to do with cows. I need a horse if you're selling."

Lyle took a short yellow pencil from a row of them in his bib pocket just to scratch his temple with the eraser.

"I'm considering pasturing Mabel. She's getting so old she practically has to deliver by the glass."

"She stand a rider?"

"Sure. A man ain't a load of full milk cans."

"I'll have a look."

The white mare was huge, with thick shaggy cannons and teeth worn down to brown stubs, but there was muscle under the loose and shifting skin. She'd do until a proper mount came along; or for that matter an ox with spirit.

"I'd sell you a stepladder if I had one," Lyle said, watching Randy make his inspection. "She's Percheron stock. That's the closest thing you'll find to royal blood around here."

"How much?"

"Ten dollars."

"I'll go six. She may be the nag queen of England, but in horse years she's older'n your old man."

"I could get eight from the dog food people in San Francisco; but my heart ain't in it. I started with Mabel and fourteen customers. She's family."

"She's barely a horse. Six."

"Make it seven and I'll throw in a pair of blinders."

"Six and you can keep the damn blinders. I ain't fixing to sell butter and cottage cheese. It's a saddle horse I'm after."

"Oh, you'll need the blinders. She wouldn't know what to do without 'em. You can kick her all day long and she'll just stand there like a knot on a fence."

"You don't know much about horse-trading, Lyle. I'm about to go down to five."

Lyle stroked the mare's broad face. "Don't you listen to him, old girl. You're going out more dignified than I will."

Randy gave him a banknote and a cartwheel dollar.

"Where's your saddle, mister?"

"I sold it in San Diego. You can't carry one and hop a freight too."

"Bareback, hey?" Lyle shook his head, stuffing the money behind the pencils. "Ride 'em, cowboy."

Mabel clopped down the wooden ramp with Randy hanging onto the reins as much to stay upright as to steer the horse. He hadn't ridden bareback in years, not since before he hurt his leg, and riding the tall mare was like sitting on the driver's seat of a stagecoach; the ground looked far away. It made him feel like a stunted boy his first time aboard.

On the road outside town he tried to spur the old girl into a trot—a gallop was too much to count on—but apart from blowing indignantly through her nostrils she showed no result, plodding at the same pace that had taken thousands of gallons of milk from door to door. For once in his life he hoped he wouldn't run into Frank. Seeing his old foe sitting a giant draft horse with blinders on might just kill him with laughing, which would be an unsatisfactory end to their contest.

He could make as good time on the soles of his own feet, but he had too much cowboy in him to choose walking when anything at all was available on four legs.

"Whoa!"

The mare, a tribute to obedience, stopped so abruptly he almost fell off. He drew the rifle from the bedroll he'd strapped across Mabel's neck and shouldered it, but held off on the trigger when he recognized Abraham Cripplehorn's Pike's Peak of a hat on the head of the man standing between the tumbledown house and barn where he'd staked his camp. A horse about half the size of Randy's stood between the traces of a two-wheeled buggy on the side of the road.

"What's that you're riding?" asked the entrepreneur as Randy approached him. "It looks like something from Homer."

"It's from Lyle, and I'll thank you not to disparage a

man's mount. You must of hit paydirt, all dressed up and renting that town rig." The man was wearing a stiff new suit, royal blue almost to the point of purple, with yellow piping, and oxblood boots with flaps over the toes. The hat was the same, but freshly blocked and brushed. He looked like the circus had gone off and left him behind.

"I have, after a fashion: a mother lode named Weber. I thought you might be running low on money for supplies and provisions." He slid a sheaf of banknotes out of his inside breast pocket.

Randy was swinging his good leg over, figuring how to drop to the ground without landing on his bad one, when something made the decision for him. It passed so close to his face that his first thought was someone had struck a match off his nose. The sound of the shot came cracking after, by which time he'd thrown himself all the way onto gravel.

NINETEEN

When your rosebush grows nothing but thorns, don't condemn your bad luck. Pierce them and sell them as needles.

"Get down, you ignorant son of a bitch."

Cripplehorn had remained standing, staring toward a line of chestnut trees to the east. When Randy, already flat on the ground, snatched the nearest ankle and jerked it out from under him, he went down hard enough on his back to knock the wind out of him. Comically, his absurd Stetson came floating down afterward like a child's handkerchief parachute.

The entrepreneur wheezed, reinflating his lungs, and rolled over onto his stomach beside Randy. "Who is it?"

"Who you think?"

"No. He wouldn't be that rash. I gave him more money just this morning."

"You tell him where I'm fixed?"

"Of course not."

"Then he followed you. The trouble with you easterners is you never turn around and look where you come from. You might as well of been borned with no swivel in your neck."

"You said there was a reward from Arizona for your capture. Maybe it's a bounty man."

"If it is he's a fool. They want me alive, which we sure won't both be if he tries to wrassle me all the way back there."

"But you said Frank would never use a rifle on you because of the unfair advantage."

"Maybe he's changed."

"I don't believe it. Yours has always been an affair of honor."

"I wouldn't put it as toney as that, but I agree it ain't like Frank. Then again, that slug missed me. Could have been just his way of announcing himself. There's one sure way to find out." He planted his palms on the ground.

"What are you doing?"

"Getting up to fetch my Ballard."

Before Cripplehorn could put words to his astonishment, Randy stood, brushed himself off, and slid the rifle from the bedroll strapped to the mare. He patted her big neck. Muscles rolled beneath his palm. "I talked you down some earlier. I'd be obliged if you'd forget it. I never had a horse stand so close to a bullet without jumping. On the other hand, maybe you're deaf."

Mabel blew again, contemptuously.

"Or lazy. I don't reckon no milk horse gets shot at regular." He checked the load in the breech, then rested the barrel across the mare's slightly swayed back. The smoke had drifted away from the trees, so he addressed the whole bunch at the top of his lungs.

"Frank, I ain't got all day!"

Silence stretched; Cripplehorn hugged the earth and wished for a hole. When the answering shout came from the trees he flinched as if it were gunfire.

"How do I know you won't plug me when I show myself? I reckon I owe you that."

"Horseshit, Frank. If you meant to put me under with that Winchester, I'd be under. So howdy right back at you."

"You're lucky I sold the rolling-block I had in Colorado. I could of shot you from there and let it fester till I caught up."

A breeze damp with bay combed the distant leaves. Then a figure appeared, moving slowly their direction, small against the towering chestnuts. A brass-action carbine dangled from one hand, muzzle pointing groundward. Randy socked the Ballard back inside the bedroll.

Curiosity got the better of Cripplehorn's sense of self-preservation. He rose to his feet, sidling until the horse and buggy stood between him and the approaching figure. After what seemed an hour, Frank Farmer stopped just inside pistol range. The tail of his frock coat was swept behind the Remington in his holster. Randy stepped out from behind the big mare.

"How do, Randy. That a horse or you shave a buffalo?"

"Shaving it weren't the hard part. The hard part was slapping on the bay rum after. I heard you taken up with a woman."

"It didn't stick. I heard you turned down the opportunity to shoot a Chinaman."

"I didn't think that was knowed outside the camp."

"I still got friends with the railroad. There ain't much to do in a roundhouse but play cards and jabber. I heard that spur went bust."

"Did it? It don't surprise me. That jasper I knocked flat with a powder keg wouldn't stop talking about the Irish going on strike. No wonder the line put up so much reward over one skinny foreman."

"It wasn't striking done it. The Apaches came back, meaner'n bloody turds. Though I can see why they'd take on so about your claiming six months' pay for one day's work; if that's what you call caving in the straw boss's head."

"It was six weeks, not months. I'm surprised it isn't ten foremen by now, and there was powder in that keg."

Frank nodded, rolling a cigarette, with the Winchester cradled in the crook of his arm. "You ready?"

"God's sake!" Cripplehorn. "You're undoing the work of years! Can't the pair of you control yourselves for two more months?"

Randy slid his Colt out of its holster, cocked it, and thumbed the cylinder around, checking his loads. "Ready."

Frank stooped to lay his carbine on the ground and

checked his Remington. When he was standing with his feet spread and the pistol hanging at his side, Randy adopted the same pose. He was raising the Colt when Abraham Cripplehorn jerked the buggy whip from its socket next to the driver's seat and, holding the ironwood handle by the whip end, hit him on the back of the head with all his might. Randy dropped, out as cold as his pistol.

BLOOD FEUD COMES TO SAN FRANCISCO.

by Jack Dodger

Randy Locke and Frank Farmer, who are well-known to these columns, brought their enmity to San Francisco yesterday when Farmer made an attempt from ambush on Locke's life.

Locke narrowly escaped death when a ball fired from cover passed within inches of his head as he was dismounting at his campsite west of Oakland.

The incident might have ended in tragedy had not an uninterested party, Abraham Titus Cripplehorn by name, took action, disabling Locke with a blow before he could return fire. His opponent, observing that the match was over for the time being, made the following statement to Cripplehorn:

"You tell that little skunk when he comes around I'll fight him anywhere, anytime, out on the desert with only the scorpions to bear witness or on stage at the Bird Cage Theatre in Tombstone."

"'Bear witness,' he said that?" Major W. B. Updegraff, resting his stiff leg on a leaf of his heaped rolltop, looked up from the pages in his hand.

"Something on that order. I wasn't taking notes at the time."

"It seems to me you hinted months ago about a public contest between Farmer and Locke. Are these desperadoes always so accommodating, to advertise your intentions in the press?"

"It isn't as if they ever made a secret of their antagonism."

"You made yourself a part of the story?"

"Fortunately I always write under a *nom de plume*. I was told once journalists should remain in the background."

"There's a simpler way." The man in the cinder-burned waistcoat found a stub of orange pencil behind one ear and scratched out the byline. "This is straight news, not human interest. I don't assign credit. I see you've annexed Oakland to San Francisco. I thought that authority belonged to the city superintendents." He struck San Francisco from the lead paragraph and crossed out the headline entirely. "I don't like it, Cripplehorn, or Dodger, or Puddin' 'n' Tame, or whatever you're calling yourself Tuesdays and Thursdays. After that first piece ran, I received a visit from a member of the Committee of Safety."

"Vigilante, I suppose."

"You suppose right, and you wouldn't be so smug about it if you were here in '77. The only reason you still see Chinese in town is there were more of them than Denis Kearney and his Pick-Handle Brigade had hickory handles. Back then it was the Tongs had the Committee running about reading the law at the end of a stick; now it's pledged to keep blood sports out of town, like cockfights and bear-baiting and public duels. If they get the notion I'm encouraging barbarism, they may just decide to bust up my press and me along with it."

"I'll take it to the *Bonanza* then, on the assumption the publisher hasn't been threatened yet." Cripplehorn held out his hand for the pages.

"People only buy Ted Sullivan's rag to start fires. I didn't say I wouldn't run it. Kearney's star has set, and this new litter skeedaddles when a cat yowls in a black alley. Even if they were a blister on the arse of the original Committee, I wouldn't let 'em tell me what I can print and what I can't. That's my name on the flag on Page Two: *W. B. Updegraff, Publisher and Editor-in-Chief.* I don't see any of their names there."

"I'm glad you see it that way. I was bluffing about Sullivan. He turned me down the first time."

"I know. He told me over whiskeys at the Bella Union after I ran it. Did you really coldcock Locke, or was it something on that order, like that Farmer quote?"

"There wasn't anything heroic to it. I hit him with a buggy whip handle when his back was turned."

The Major showed yellow teeth around his cigar stump.

"Too bad Kearney didn't know you five years ago. He

drafted the city ordinance against carrying firearms, but he liked his bludgeons."

"It's a pleasure doing business with you, Major. When I've made all the arrangements I'll place a full-page advertisement in the *Spar.*"

"Like hell you will. I don't approve of your design any more than the Committee. If you come in here waving money in my face promoting murder, I'll throw you out through my one and only window."

TWENTY

The success of any venture is measured by the size and number of obstacles overcome.

Cripplehorn had said nothing to Frank while Randy was senseless. Where reason was missing, recriminations accomplished nothing. Frank withdrew, leaving the entrepreneur to await Randy's awakening.

"What in hell did you hit me with?" He sat up, feeling gingerly the knot on the back of his head.

"Does it matter?" Cripplehorn was seated on the driver's seat of the buggy, drinking peach brandy from a silver-and-pigskin flask.

"Where is he?"

"Gone."

"Gone where?"

"Why, so you can finish what he started? I always heard you cowboys were as good as your word."

"Talk to him. He's the one broke it."

"As would you have, given the opportunity. You two are worse than a philandering husband. He can't keep his pecker in his pants and you can't keep those hoglegs in their holsters. I'm splitting you up until the time of the contest."

"Where you sending me?"

"I'm putting you up at the Asiatic for now. The reporters will be looking for you at the Palace and the Eldorado. I know how that annoys you."

"Hell, I thought you was going to say South America or somesuch place."

"Frank's the one broke the bargain. I'm sending him out of the state until I can get things worked out in Sacramento. There will be resistance, but I'm counting on Weber's money to soften it up."

But secrecy was a luxury infamy could not afford. An old acquaintance from his cowhand days recognized Frank on a railroad platform in Boise, and by the time his train crossed into Montana Territory, reporters were gathering at every station clamoring for his comments. He avoided them by staying aboard until the engine gushed to a stop in the mining town of Butte, where he stepped down carrying his valise and his Winchester in its scabbard.

"Frank, you running away from Randy?" asked an unpressed gentleman of the press from Chicago.

"Say that again and I'll drop you where you stand."

The representative from the *Billings Gazette* asked him if it was true he intended to shoot Randy in broad daylight in public.

"I'd shoot him in the dark if I could see in it."

"Aren't you concerned you'll be arrested for murder?"

Frank, bathed, brushed, and barbered, smiled in appreciation at this vision from the *Omaha Herald,* a trim young woman in a becoming traveling suit and a flower patch on her straw hat. Spots of color appeared on her cheeks.

"I'll cross that crick when it counts."

The reporter from the local *Miner,* in pinstripe suit and stovepipe boots, asked him what he thought of Butte.

"I'll let you know once I find it under all this muck." Every surface in sight bore traces of smoke from the smelting plants: A finger left a track through the grime.

"Where are you stopping?" asked the same journalist.

"Someplace clean, I hope."

"Good luck with that."

Frank registered at the Copper Palace, a four-story hotel decorated almost entirely with material from the local mine: The ceiling in the lobby was made up of pressed sheets of copper, all the hardware and even the chandelier were copper, and copper covered the desk, behind which stood a clerk who might have been fashioned from the same reddish metal, although this was probably an illusion created by reflection from all that copper. That evening Frank dined in the hotel restaurant with the comely female reporter from Nebraska Territory, who after he said his good byes in a voice that carried, followed him up to his room as the waiters were clearing the tables.

"Abraham Cripplehorn?"

The entrepreneur took in the small, fussily dressed man standing outside the open door of his room at the Palace. On his waistcoat hung a brass star attached by tiny chains to an engraved plate containing his title of office. "You have the advantage, sir."

"I'm Connie Post, sheriff of San Mateo County. I'm here to serve you."

"How very generous."

The irony of this response found no purchase on the little man's spade-bearded face. He handed the guest a roll of parchment covered with Spencerian script and embossed with a seal.

"This is an injunction, signed by Judge Webster Bennett, prohibiting you or anyone else from conducting a murderous exhibition in this county. You've been served."

"Indeed I have. Bennett, you said?"

"Webster Bennett, district judge."

"Thank you."

That individual, horse-faced with white sidewhiskers combed out to shoulder width, entertained Cripplehorn from behind the desk in his chambers in a county courthouse dripping with limestone gewgaws and bronze statuary, some grafter's dream of wealth come to life. The glass eyes of antelope heads stared down from the walls. Going by his obvious threescore and ten, the jurist had bagged the creatures back when San Francisco was still in swaddling clothes.

"Don't think I'm ungrateful for your offer, Mr. Cripplehorn. I'm retiring at the end of this term and do not intend to seek reelection. Mr. Cable, the prosecuting attorney, is running for my party, but he isn't in a position to reverse the injunction I ordered. Any donation from you would come entirely from your interest in good government."

Appeals were telegraphed to all the other counties in California. Some were rejected by return wire, others after local debate attended by concerned citizens, many of them women. ("Supporters of the event should not hold their husbands accountable for opposing it," wrote the correspondent from the *Examiner*. "Faced with overwhelming numbers, a wise general withdraws from the field.") Still others were considering the request when Sacramento intervened:

By order of the Governor of California, no contest involving humans that is designed to conclude in the death or serious injury of one or more of the participants shall take place anywhere in the state. Any attempt to stage such an exhibition will be met with the full weight of the law. The state militia is hereby

ORDERED TO STAND READY TO DEFEND IT, IF NECESSARY WITH DEADLY FORCE.

"Please correct me if I'm mistaken in my understanding of this proclamation," Cripplehorn told the press in the conference room at the Palace. "Is it the governor's intention to prevent killing by killing?"

Badinage, however, was ineffective, and after conferring with Sheridan Weber ("Don't ask me about politics, Abe; I haven't voted since Grant"), the entrepreneur looked into substitute venues.

However, no sooner did the news enter the telegraph columns than representatives of the neighboring states and territories declared that they would not host so callous a display of savagery. Oregon, Nevada, Arizona, and Utah warned that all three principals would face arrest the moment they crossed their borders.

"Arizona wasted its breath," Randy said. "It's my neck to visit the place anyway."

The rest of the country followed suit. In the governor's office in Albany, New York, Grover Cleveland signed a bill banning the event by name, thc first law in that state's history aimed directly at three U.S. citizens in particular.

Cripplehorn was indignant. "This kind of thing wouldn't have been possible before the Rebellion."

Randy was bemused. "I wisht my old man was alive. He'd be proud to think his son had been declared war on all on his own."

"We just lost Rhode Island in the *Bulletin.*"

"We lost Delaware and Ohio in the *Call.* I'm almost afraid to look at the *Examiner.*"

"I can't see why you find this so amusing."

"You're the one wants to be the Cornelius Vanderbilt of gunning folks. All I want is Frank in the ground, and that always was against the law."

Mexico and Canada came next. Under pressure from Washington, President Diaz mobilized the *federales* to turn Cripplehorn & Company back at the Rio Grande. Ottawa, not to be outdone by the rest of North America, announced that the Northwest Mounted Police would eject them from the Dominion of Canada as undesirable aliens. In Butte, Frank bought a round of drinks for some journalists and remarked that he felt downright hurt: "I never wanted to go till they told me I couldn't. Now I got a hankering to ride up there and shoot some moose, and maybe a Mountie or two. I seen a picture once of British soldiers in a history book. Those red shirts make an easy target."

Unlike Randy, "the dandified gentleman from Texas" not only didn't mind the attention, but sought it out. He couldn't stand five minutes at a bar waiting for someone to recognize him without identifying himself, and didn't have to pay for a drink the rest of the visit. He bought a new suit and a pair of boots with fancy flaps like he'd admired on Cripplehorn, had a gunsmith replace the old cracked grips on his Remington with ivory ones, and had just left the shop when his gaze fell upon a frame building with photographs on display in the front window.

> *Butte, M.T., September l6*—Mr. Frank Farmer, the notorious Southwestern gun man, had his picture struck last week in O. C. Nordstrom's studio on Silver Bow Street last week. He posed before a Swiss alpine backdrop with pistol and rifle on display, and most who have seen it agree that he is a fine figure of a man for an assassin. Straightaway several of the local citizenry offered to buy prints of his likeness for souvenirs, and by the end of the week they were selling for a quarter apiece. It is rumored that should the mines play out, the city fathers can increase revenue by inviting all of the celebrated frontier pistoleers to come in and have their likenesses made for sale to tourists.

"That's something you and I should consider." Cripplehorn looked up from the telegraph column in the *Bulletin* at Randy, stretched out in his sock feet on his bed in the Asiatic. "All the famous bad men have sat at one time or another. People would take it against your reputation if you don't."

"How do I know you won't sell it to the papers?"

"They can't usc them; they bleed, Updegraff says. The paper's too coarse and absorbent."

"You asked him."

"We can't all hole up in a hotel breaking wind all day. Someone has to keep up the momentum."

"I ain't doing it. Some son of a bitch in Arizona's sure to put it on a shinplaster and double the reward on account of I'm famous."

"You get more mileage out of that old business than any bounty man. For all you say about disliking the attention, I think you enjoy being wanted."

"Well, I don't like reporters. They ask impertinent questions and they all smell like moldy cardboard."

Randy was using the name George Purdy, borrowed from the mule-headed Circle X foreman who'd fired him for shooting Frank the first time and leaving the outfit shy one man; thereby doubling the deficit. He was unwilling to leave the hotel except to walk the stiffness out of his leg, and then only after dark. But in the midst of all the world telling him how unwelcome he and Frank and Cripplehorn were, he got restless and went out for a ride, looking all around for journalists when he exited out a side door and keeping his head down with the brim of his old weather-stained hat obscuring his features.

The man who operated the Golden Gate Livery left off his whittling and said, "That horse of yours died last night. You owe me for a week plus the cost of dragging out the carcass."

Randy went into the stall to see for himself. Old Mabel lay on her side with her eyes gone glassy and flies crawling on her.

He patted her side. "Damn if I ain't sorry. I used you for a shooting stand and you didn't even blink. The army lost a good mount when they hooked you to a damn milk wagon." He went back out and asked how much to put her under.

"There's a dog food place downtown'd give you cash for it."

Randy gave him a banknote. "I'll be asking 'em if they bought an old white mare from the Golden Gate Livery. If the answer ain't no I'll come back and kill you."

> *San Francisco, Sept. 22*—The Spanish governor of Cuba has informed the U.S. State Department that he will arrest anyone intending to stage a blood duel in his jurisdiction. This is undoubtedly a reference to the Messrs. Locke, Farmer, and Cripplehorn, whose search for an arena in which to work out the fatal differences between the first two men has appeared regularly in these columns. With President Arthur having banned the contest from these United States, this brings to a total of four countries, thirteen individual states, and eight territories to declare they would not host so callous a display of savagery. The editors of the *Examiner* note that the principles of the good Christian faith still prevail in these uncertain times.

Asked by reporters over liquor and sandwiches in Cripplehorn's suite in the Palace if this latest blow meant the end of his plans, the promoter smiled. "The Cubans sacrifice a bullfighter every few months and I've never heard a word of protest from Santiago. Still, it's a big old world."

"Are you saying you're taking the show abroad like Buffalo Bill?" asked the man from the *Call,* around a mouthful of liverwurst.

"I can't take the risk of putting Locke and Farmer on the same boat. I'd rather avoid the complication of arranging separate crossings with so many other preparations to be made."

"Where, then?" The *Chicago Tribune.*

Cripplehorn swallowed peach brandy and responded with two words.

"The Strip."

TWENTY-ONE

Education begins with books and instruction and ends with travel. It is a rolling classroom.

I suppose some desperadoes, all tucked into their hideout beds, say their prayers before sleeping. Contrary to the assumptions of the editors of the *San Francisco Examiner,* there are Christians on the run from justice. When a damned soul prays, I don't reckon God ever gave him a more satisfactory answer than the Cherokee Strip.

Although I'm no more an authority on how the Congress works than the senators and representatives themselves, I imagine the discussion went something like this:

THE HON. CONSTANT FLAPDOODLE: What do we do with that piece of the Indian Nations? It just kind of sticks out like a gingham patch on a Sunday shirt.

SEN. EVERLASTING PETTIFOG: What's it got? Gold, silver, timber?

FLAPDOODLE: Just red clay and scrub, far as I can tell.

SEN. FENCE STRADDLER: How come we ain't give it to the injuns?

FLAPDOODLE: Which tribe? We divvied up the rest of the territory among 'em.

PETTIFOG: Hell, let's just toss it up in the air and let the bastards fight over it amongst themselves.

FLAPDOODLE: Makes sense to me. Second the motion.

FENCE STRADDLER: All in favor?

It was a rectangular slice of the Indian Nations, about the size of Greece. As to woods and prairie and rocky outcrop, it was a fair example of the rest of the frontier. Flapdoodle, Pettifog, and Straddler didn't know it from darkest Africa. Declaring it the communal property of the area tribes meant it was officially unassigned, the only piece of the United States left up for grabs, and therefore no one's property at all. It stood outside the law, federal, territorial, and local, which made it a bolt-hole for every wanted fugitive in America.

The fugitives took notice. Before Fence Straddler's gavel stopped ringing, the Strip filled fit to bust with murderers, rapists, wife-beaters, train robbers, and common road agents who'd worn out their welcome everywhere else in the civilized world except on scaffolds. Since there was no reason to lay low with no one looking for them, they helped themselves to whatever was handy and seldom left witnesses. The grittiest of U.S. marshals hesitated to go there except in armed convoys. Policemen appointed from among the Five Civilized Tribes—Cherokee, Creek, Seminole, Choctaw, and Chickasaw—done their damnedest to keep order, but their authority was limited and they were scattered like buckshot.

An army fort might have helped contain the atrocities. However, through an agreement between the Indians and Washington that no one really understood, the military was banned from the territory. In any case, there was no precedent for the cavalry protecting Indians from United States citizens; generally the situation was opposite. It was No Man's Land, utterly lawless.

Where better, Cripplehorn reasoned, to stage an outlaw entertainment?

"It's a fair piece off," said Randy, "and aboard a hot train. Where's Frank stand on the matter?"

"I wired him in Montana. He asked the same question about you."

"Hell, I'd go clean to China to have it out with him for the last time."

"I felt certain you would. I answered him along those lines, and he said just what you did; only in his case it was Russia."

"I'm surprised you didn't just crack us both on the head like you done me in Oakland and dump us aboard a fast freight."

"There are a thousand things to be done. I haven't time to waste running back and forth carrying messages. There's no telling when Washington might change its mind and annex the Strip, placing it under civil authority."

"Can we stop on the way for a bottle of Old Pepper? That fruity horse piss of yours gives me the two-step worse than cooking grease."

It was a hot ride as predicted, and hotter still as they chugged down the eastern side of the Divide and stopped in Pueblo, a town noted for its salubrious climate—but not in September—to take on water. Randy sat in a wallow of sweat, screwing up his face against the glare through his window, and allowed as how he'd had his life's portion of dusty towns, burnt grain served up as coffee, and sour women.

Cripplehorn got up from the seat beside him. "I won't be a moment."

"What for, you want to borrow a cup of dust?"

"I need to send a telegram."

"Give Frank my regards and tell him to keep breathing till I get there."

"He's already on his way. I'll fill you in later."

Randy felt he was in the Nations before he saw the place: a brief whiff of brimstone, a tightening in the chest, a sickness in the stomach carried by old miseries not necessarily his. The territory had been born in tears and irrigated by them ever since.

Then again, he might simply have been train sick.

"You've been staring out that window for miles," Cripplehorn said. "What's wrong?"

He turned his head away. "My mother said I had injun blood back on her side; Iroquois, I think she said. I reckon some great-great grandpappy just walked acrosst my grave."

"It never occurred to me you had a mother."

"She died when I was fourteen and I ran away."

"Because of your father?"

"No. We never met."

"You're lucky."

In the town of Cimarron, named after the river separating the white and red territories, the entrepreneur excused himself again. The place was built of new yellow wood just waiting for a spark to come along and burn it to the ground. Randy watched through the window as Cripplehorn shook hands with a fat man in a suit too heavy for the climate and a hat with a rolled brim, bright metal doodads dangling from his watch chain. He accepted a cigar from a battery of them in the man's breast pocket, wagged his chin little, and nodded lots. From his gold-cornered wallet Cripplehorn slid a fistful of banknotes, folded them into a little square, and shook the man's hand again, coming away with nothing in his. He got back on board just as the whistle blasted its first warning.

"We're stopping here." He took his carpetbag down from the overhead rack and reached for Randy's bedroll.

"Don't touch my gear." Randy sprang up and fetched it himself. "What's in Cimarron, besides a dose of clap?"

"Our home, for the time being. It's all arranged. We've got a two-month lease on a farmer's field not two minutes from here."

"What we fixing to put in, oats or potatoes?"

"Neither. Planting's done. I just sealed the deal with the banker who foreclosed on the place. He's the one I sent the telegram to from Pueblo, to arrange this meeting. The Choctaw who worked it put in corn, but the hot summer burned up his investment: The stalks grew tall enough, but the kernels wouldn't form, and he ran out of extensions."

"I don't know why he thought he could raise anything in this country."

"Just a cry of despair. We're going to plow under what's left and stake a great big tent to discourage freeloaders."

"Whose working the plow, you?"

"The farmer himself. Banker Anderson says he's willing to do it, and whatever other odd jobs come up, just for letting him and his family stay in the house through the winter."

"And I reckon his wife will knit us the tent."

"That's the beauty of the plan. We'll sell advertising on the canvas, inside and out. With the house we're expecting, any smart merchant would chase us all the way down the street to stuff our pockets in return for space. It will cover our overhead and more."

"We're selling empty space?"

"That's how it works."

"I'll be damned."

"That's foreordained."

"Don't leases and such need signing papers? I didn't see nothing change hands but cash money."

"It's that kind of deal. A case might be made for conspiracy should the situation change. A trail of paper could prove an embarrassment."

"Well, we wouldn't want to embarrass a banker. How do you know he won't crawfish?"

"That part called for diplomacy. I reminded him there would likely be one gun man left standing when the thing was done. That whole business of honor among western gentlemen has always been based on the lead standard."

"You draw me and Frank like a gun."

Cripplehorn fixed him with his good eye; though Randy had the strange impression there was life in the one carved from ivory, cold as it was. "You were what you are before I met you both. Don't pretend I'm worse than either one of you."

The whistle shrilled twice as the train prepared to pull out.

"I ain't renting no place with you, if that's what you're thinking."

Out on the platform, Cripplehorn stopped and turned. Randy leered.

"Didn't think I knew about that, did you? Frisco's nothing more than small towns all bunched together. Folks talk. Frank must of got soft not to of shot you weeks ago. I almost done it on sight last year."

The promoter raised his voice above the plunging pistons, holding down his hat against the suction of the departing train. "It's not the Palace, or even the Asiatic. The Cherokee Rest is the best Cimarron has to offer."

"As opposed to what else? I didn't count but four blocks, counting the town pump."

"A boarding house or two, but there's no privacy there. I can't promise a private bath or even hot water, but there won't be any false eyelashes in the basin."

"I'm sorry to hear that. It was my only female companionship that whole time. What about Frank?"

"Oh, I'm putting him up in an adjoining room so I can sleep in the crossfire." Cripplehorn mounted the steps of a wooden front porch and opened a door, jingling a set of sleigh bells strung from the inside knob.

Dust motes hung motionless in the sunlight slanting in through the front window. A squaw rug, most of its color gone, lay on a plank floor and the moth-eaten head of a boar tusker glared down from the wall above the stairs.

A loud smack sent Randy groping for his Colt. Then he saw a clerk scraping a dead fly off a rolled-up newspaper against the edge of the desk. He let his hand fall from the pistol.

"Wherever he is, it better not be no Eldorado, that's all I got to say."

TWENTY-TWO

The theater's unrespectable reputation is undeserved. The amount of labor and dedication involved in preparing a production is a test of character.

The dilemma of what to do with Frank was as vexing as any of the arrangements necessary to ensure the success of Crip's Folly, as the press had christened the enterprise. (It was coined by John Clum, editor of the *Tombstone Epitaph,* as a way of drawing fire away from that city's sinister recent history, and spread from paper to paper like smallpox.) Wherever he wound up, his inability to resist attention was bound to announce his whereabouts, and the situation had increased to the point where anywhere in the Nations was too close.

The solution was so simple it's no wonder a confidence man whose train of thought ran in twisted circles took so long arriving at it: Cripplehorn told Frank to stay put. He could hold court in the Copper Palace as much as he wanted, and distance alone would prevent Randy's native impatience from boiling over.

The reporter who covered the Strip for the *Fort Smith Elevator* was a bandy-legged rooster with a horse-collar beard who looked like Walt Whitman and swore like Jo Shelby. He wore an out-at-the-elbows morning coat, Confederate trousers with a stripe, and a Union forage cap. He was a veteran war correspondent whose thirst for action had led him down to Mexico to cover the revolution, and when that ended too soon he'd come back north and traveled from one boomtown journal to the next, mostly on foot, before finding satisfaction in the worst part of the Nations. None of his colleagues would willingly roam those caves and thickets poking into other folks' affairs, so he enjoyed a freedom of movement unprecedented in his profession.

Caleb Munch interviewed Abraham Cripplehorn in his room overlooking Cimarron's main street. The visitor sat in the room's only chair with his legs crossed. It was hard to tell where his limbs left off and the spindle legs started. His subject sat on the bed with his back propped against a pillow and his legs stretched out in front of him to keep his trouser creases straight. He was smoking the cigar he'd gotten from banker Anderson.

"You spend most of your time separating your clients like a couple of fighting cocks," Munch said.

"More like a pair of unruly children, which is worse. Where is your notebook?"

"I kept losing them, so now I just remember." Munch was an unsmiling man who had no patience with humor, a clutter in speech as it was in written copy. "You stand to sacrifice your whole investment if Locke and Farmer tangle too soon."

"Is that a question?"

"I never ask them. Around here you get out of the habit."

"Doesn't that make it hard for you to conduct an interview?"

"It hasn't yet."

"These next three weeks will be the most difficult. But the closer we get to the event, the easier it will be to keep them under control. They've been out to kill each other so long, another day shouldn't matter. Tempers tend to cool when money becomes imminent."

"I've yet to read a word about why they're so determined to destroy each other."

"I've asked, but all I ever got was a glib answer. I think they've forgotten themselves. They've been at it so long I don't suppose it matters."

"No one's ever explained what a dog has in mind when it chases a cat. You know, Cripplehorn, people compare you to those blood-crazy Roman emperors. There are other ways to make a living."

"Not for me. Not the way I want to live."

"I want to sit down with Locke."

"I don't advise it. Reporters rank just below Farmer on his list."

Munch untangled himself from the chair. "I think I'll knock on his door. You don't object."

"I never step between another man and a mistake."

Fort Smith, Oct. 1—Caleb Munch, our correspondent in the Indian Nations, inquired of Randolph Locke, the prominent duellist, as to the nature of his antipathy toward Frank Farmer, also of that profession. He was unable to obtain an answer, but both Munch and Locke are recovering at present from injuries sustained during the interview.

"I got thirty-one bad teeth, and that fellow with the whiskers knocked out the good one." Randy, standing with his braces down before the mirror above the washbasin in his room, inspected the gap. His upper lip was puffed up twice normal size and he had sixteen stitches above his right eye, swollen also.

"How'd he get that close?" Cripplehorn asked.

"I opened the door to shoo him out and he hit me square in the mouth."

"Where was your gun?"

"I dropped it out of pure astonishment. Nobody's crazy enough to hit a man holding a pistol."

"I saw him coming out after the commotion. He had a sleeve torn off and there was blood in his beard."

"Next time it'll be a slug in his chest. Maybe not, though. It's bad luck to kill a crazy man."

The tent was the biggest thing the local wagon-sheet maker had ever attempted. He stitched together most of his stock, solving the problem of waterproofing by overlapping and understitching, and staked it out in the field where the exhibition was scheduled for the printer to stencil the advertising. When a team of laborers erected it, it stood taller than any building in town and encompassed almost the entire plowed patch of ground. Trumpeted the *Elevator*:

DEATH TENT BIGGER THAN
CODY'S WILD WEST.

Locke *v.* Farmer

Arena Compares to Madison Square Garden.

Largest Construction in the Nations.

"Blood Coliseum," Declares the Hon. Isaac Parker.

Our Famous Jurist Decries

Official Inefficacy to Prevent Barbarous Display.

A squad of carpenters abandoned construction of an Episcopal church to build bleachers for the spectators, who could read of the miraculous properties of Edison's Elixir, consider the Blue Plate Special at the Kickapoo House, admire a giant shoe illustrating the wares of Gabriel & Sons, Cobblers, and ponder the marble monuments available from C.C. Cox, Stonecutter. There were notices printed on both sides of the canvas.

Cripplehorn spent more time with the printer than anyone else. He had tickets made with legal waivers on the backs, indemnifying the exhibitors against damages in the event of injury or death as the result of a stray bullet, and designed posters to be placed in every shopkeeper's window for miles around (EXHIBITION OF THE CENTURY! A DUEL TO THE DEATH! FRANK FARMER AND RANDY LOCKE, TOGETHER FOR THE LAST TIME! NOV. 10, 1882. TICKETS $1.00 [ONE DOLLAR] Jack Dodger, Programme Director).

"What kind of stock?" asked the printer, holding the sheet scribbled by his customer.

"Something that will take this." Cripplehorn handed him a stiff-backed photograph of Frank, looking the proper bad man with his ivory-handled Remington poking above his belt and the butt-plate of his Winchester planted on the floor, the Matterhorn for some reason in the background.

"Take good care of it. I had to send for it all the way from California. I want Farmer's name underneath in twelve-point type. I've been spending a lot of time with newspapermen, and know the lingo."

"What about the other one?"

"He's camera shy. Do what you can with this."

The printer took the wanted poster with the bad sketch of Randy. "This reward still good?"

"It won't be after the tenth."

TWENTY-THREE

Philosophy is just another word for regret.

Frank's train got in late. The station was dark, and the few people left to greet the passengers looked like phantoms in the light leaking from the windows of the coaches.

"What happened?" said Cripplehorn.

"Tree fell across the tracks forty miles back. We sat in the dark two hours waiting for the crew to chop it loose. Some folks will do anything to keep this here extravaganza from happening."

"Impossible. No one knew you were on the train."

"I sort of let it slip in Billings. I reckon there was a fellow or two from the press mixed in amongst the regulars. News sure spreads these days. Hard to believe it took a month for some to hear Lincoln got shot."

"Just out of curiosity, what would it take to make you keep your mouth shut?"

"Hell, I thought you'd be pleased. You spent most of our

stake advertising this shindig. I got you the same thing and it didn't cost a cent. Where's Randy?"

There was no reason not to tell him. The Cherokee Rest had been in all the papers after Randy's interview with Caleb Munch. "In the hotel. He gave me his word he'd stay away from you until the day after tomorrow. I want yours. Thirty-six hours, that's all I ask."

"I stayed in jail longer than that. I reckon I can wait a day and a half out of sixteen years."

"Your word?"

"You got it."

"Seems to me I had it once before. You know how that turned out."

Teeth flashed in Frank's whiskers. "You ever broke a bone?"

Cripplehorn touched his cheekstrap, an involuntary gesture. "Yes."

"Then you know oncet one's broke and knitted back together it's stronger than it was."

"You westerners and your homilies. You can't shoot the moon, it's unlikely you'll ever see an elephant, and a promise isn't a bone." He shook his head. "I never will understand this regional concept of honor, especially when it might get you killed."

"That's easy. You go back on it, you're kilt for sure."

They stopped before a shallow two-story house, whitewashed with green trim. BED AND BOARD read a wooden sign suspended from the porch roof. It was dark but for a coal-oil lamp burning in a ground-floor window with a furious moth batting at the glass.

Cripplehorn said, "I took the precaution of arranging a separate accommodation. I hope you're not offended. I've played the percentages all my life, and human nature being what it is—"

"The trouble with you slick talkers is the words come too fast and too many." Frank shoved his valise into the other's arms. "You carry it the rest of the way. I'm as tuckered out as if I was swinging an axe right alongside that crew."

"You'd better get your rest. And go easy on the whiskey. That legal waiver won't stand up in court if an innocent bystander stops a bullet fired by a drunk who can't shoot straight."

Frank shook his head. "There ain't no such thing as innocent bystanders."

"I'm curious about the Swiss backdrop." Caleb Munch crossed his legs in a bent-arm rocking chair, circles of sticking-plaster on his forehead, one cheek, and a pink patch shaved out of his beard. He looked like Walt Whitman after a run-in with John L. Sullivan. He showed Frank the photograph from Butte.

"It was hot. My boots was so full of sweat they squished when I walked. The fellow with the camera kept pulling down canvas sheets from rollers, asking which I liked.

When I got to that one it was like a north breeze. Greek temples sure didn't do it, nor palm trees on a pile of sand."

"I don't suppose you'd care to tell me what it is about Randy Locke gets your back up."

"I ain't just sure, only I took a dislike to him the minute we laid eyes on each other. Hell, you catch my loop. I read where you went to get his story and wound up dancing with him Texas style."

"I'm conducting this interview. Not liking a man seems a poor reason for murder."

"It wouldn't be murder. We neither of us never made a play without warning and without both of us was heeled."

"Cripplehorn says in Oakland you shot at Locke from cover, without announcing yourself first."

"That *was* the announcement. It was to get his attention."

"Readers of the *Elevator* will need some assurance of that."

"Hell, he's alive, ain't he?"

"Old Gideon." Cripplehorn stood the quart bottle on the pinewood chest of drawers. "It's the closest thing to sipping whiskey you can get down the street. Did you know saloons are illegal in the Nations? Not that it matters in the Strip, where everything's so far outside the law it's a law unto itself. Just tonight I've seen two men threatened with death and had to sprint to avoid being tackled and raped by a lewd woman who'd dress out at three hundred pounds."

"I know Maude. You should of let her catch up." Randy, busy with one hand disassembling his Colt on the nightstand, pulled the cork with his teeth and spat it in the general direction of nowhere. "Want a snort?"

"Lord, no. The last time I drank liquor that hard I woke up in Juarez with a burro in my bed."

"I hope it was a jenny. How bad's the news? Every time I get a gift from you it costs me."

"I want you to pose for a photograph."

"We had this conversation. You just wasted the price of a bottle."

"Hear me out. That half-ass sketch of you in Arizona must have been made by a demented child. The proof the printer showed me demonstrated the contrast. It was ludicrous. Surely you want to come off as well as Frank."

"I will and more, oncet he's in hell."

"You haven't heard the rest."

"There's more?" He took a swig, put down the bottle, and thrust a pipe cleaner through a chamber. The acidy stench of the solvent warped the air in his room.

"I want you to pose with Frank."

Randy paused in mid-thrust. Then he chuckled.

"You got yourself a deal, Mr. Cripplehorn. I never miss an opportunity to catch up with Frank."

"There's one condition."

"There usually is, and mostwise more than one." He extracted the pipe cleaner and blew through the chamber. A low whistle resulted.

"No loads in your weaponry. I've petitioned the town council for a deputy marshal to be on hand to inspect it."

Randy finished his cleaning and started in with the oil. A pleasant scent of vanilla took the edge off the acrid odor of the solvent.

"Hell. I was afraid you'd have me strip to the skin in case I had a belly gun stuck up my ass."

Cripplehorn reacted as he usually did once his fish was on the hook; pushing his luck. "You'll need a new wardrobe. That hat of yours wouldn't even make a good bucket, filled with holes as it is, and your trousers look like a band of gypsies moved out of them."

"My hat keeps the sun off my skull and the pants cover my ass. That's as much as any man can ask of his personal gear."

"You're right, I suppose. Frank ordered himself a new suit of clothes from Montgomery Ward, and a bootmaker named Bluewater is fixing him up with a custom pair made from the indigenous cottonmouth. He'll come off a clown next to you in your honest rags."

Randy started putting the Colt back together. He paused to pull from the bottle.

"I won't wear a chimney tile like Ben Thompson, nor a beetle hat like that dude Luke Short. Maybe a good Texas crown with a plain band, and a coat that don't make me look like a tinhorn or an undertaker. I reckon I could use a new pair of boots. Bluewater, you say his name was?"

"Still is, I imagine."

"Well, I sure don't want no snake; its mate might come looking for him. There's a yard or two of buffler hide left, I wouldn't mind wearing it. Them shaggies kept me in tall corn."

Cripplehorn felt that old orgasmic thrill of conquest, head to toe. "I'll ask."

The camera was a big wooden box propped on a steel tripod in a small studio smelling of caustic chemicals, with men's and women's clothes hanging from a pipe rack on casters, hats enough to open a haberdashery, a forest of walking sticks in a bamboo umbrella stand, and various items of weaponry from a Confederate officer's sabre to a large-bore rifle that fired elephant rounds; although many of those who booked a session provided their own costumes and props. One wall was covered with pictures of grim-faced wedded couples, firemen gathered around pump wagons, a locomotive laboring up a grade, and a twister, a spectacular composition.

The photographer, a young Osage named Andrew Fox, ducked under his black cloth to inspect the focus. Refracting mirrors gave him an image of two men suspended upside down, one in an upholstered chair with a floral print, the other standing beside the chair with one hand resting on the back.

Randy and Frank had watched the Osage pulling down landscapes painted on canvas attached to rollers, rejecting a pagan temple in Rome, palm trees, Versailles, and the Pacific Ocean before agreeing on a meadow shaded by tall oaks.

"Looks right peaceful," Randy said.

Frank said, "I clumb trees just like them back in Pennsylvania."

"Too bad you didn't fall out of one and bust your neck."

"Gentlemen," said Cripplehorn, in a warning tone, nodding toward the two off-duty city deputies he'd hired to observe the session. They stood at opposite ends of the room, wearing heavy-handled Colts in stiff holsters. One had a ten-gauge shotgun broken open over the crook of one arm.

"You said there'd be just one. We got no rounds." Randy bit off the words.

"That bowie of yours is too picturesque to leave out, but it's more than just a stage property. I know about Frank's clasp knife."

"That's just for whittling," Frank said. "We don't settle our scores with cutlery. We ain't Mexicans."

"These men are here merely to protect you both from those base instincts we all possess in some form."

Frank said, "I never been insulted in such pretty words."

As the shorter man, Randy posed standing, wearing a stiff new Texas pinch hat, a striped waistcoat over a lawn shirt with plain garters gathering the sleeves, and whipcord trousers tucked inside knee-length glossy brown boots, his worn old spurs on the heels. His Colt hung in his soft leather holster and he held his Ballard with the stock resting on the floor. Frank, in his new suit, fancy flap-toed boots, and tall-crowned sugar-loaf sombrero, sat with his Winchester across his lap. Both flinched when Andrew Fox raised a hod heaped with magnesium powder and touched it off with a candle, plunging the room into bright dazzle followed by acrid smoke; but the shutter was faster than even their reflexes, capturing them in the moment, calm and resolute.

For a time, the original plate was on display among other assorted hardcases in a museum in Guthrie, but it was destroyed in a fire soon after Teddy Roosevelt turned the Indian Nations into the State of Oklahoma. But you can still find a print in a junk store if you're looking, or pick up one of the posters Cripplehorn had made, all curling and flyspecked with the faces faded to blank ovals.

You can get a good price, too. The men are forgotten now, like the buffalo and the Great Plains Wolf and the range where they all wandered.

TWENTY-FOUR

Avoid cards and spirits, or stand in the crossfire of ruin.

The day of the event, Abraham Cripplehorn sat at a campaign table in front of the gargantuan tent with several rolls of tickets and a strongbox, the off-duty deputies posted to see no one ran off with either. He set up at 9:00 A.M. and by noon had sold out, with two hours to go before the tent opened for business. There wasn't a room to be had in Cimarron, whose streets were filled with strange horses and buckboards and carriages from throughout the territory and places beyond. He'd hired a brass band made up of volunteer firemen and a talented local stock clerk to juggle bright rubber balls to open the show.

At quarter to two, Cripplehorn sent the two deputies to escort the featured players from their rooms. He inspected his new gold watch several times, listening to the band playing "The Garryowen," before the deputies returned without them.

The Rusty Bucket Saloon operated openly and illegally on the south side of the tracks, where from time to time a satisfied customer was run over by the Katy Flyer while weaving across the rails. It was the original railroad station before the new brick one was built on the north side, a fine solid construction of lath-and-plaster, and long enough to accommodate a paneled mahogany bar and scrolled backbar that had been brought in, dismantled, in freight wagons before the coming of the railroad. It offered two gaming tables with green baize tops and steel-engraved pictures in frames chronicling the triumphs of George Washington. The owner was an Irishman married to a Creek woman, who bought his stock from whiskey runners who managed to elude Judge Parker's marshals by entering the territory directly from the west and north without crossing their jurisdiction.

Today it was deserted except for the Irishman and a short-coupled customer in new clothes with a Colt on his hip. Everyone else, apparently, was either in Cripplehorn's big tent or on his way there to take in the show.

"You're fixing to be late, Mr. Locke," said the man behind the bar, a fine-boned example of lace-curtain stock who kept order in the place with two feet of billiard cue and a shotgun nearly as short.

Randy directed his scowl first to the bartender, then to the poster with his and Frank's picture on it propped up in the front window. "Well, they can't start the ball without me." He thumped his glass twice on the bar. The man came his way with a bottle and filled it to the top. "You know this John Barleycorn doesn't mix with shooting."

"You might be right. I disremember even asking you for the advice."

"Holy Jesus, Mary, and Joseph." The bartender stood with the bottle in one hand and the cork in the other, staring at Frank coming in the door.

"Well, if they weren't in their rooms, you should've gone looking for them," Cripplehorn said. "The town isn't that big."

One of the off-duty deputies, tall and rangy with handlebars and a little paintbrush beard, moved a plug from one cheek to the other. "My mama didn't raise me to go looking for no puma in no thicket. You wanted 'em to stay put, you should of posted guards at their doors."

"The marshal didn't have any more men to spare and I don't trust civilians I don't know. Find them. Please."

"That's better. It's a little-bitty word, don't cost nothing, and does so much." He loosened his pistol in its holster, looked at his partner, and jerked his head over his shoulder. The other deputy, a Chickasaw half-breed with deep pockmarks on his face, slammed shut the breech of his ten-gauge and they moved off away from the brumping band inside and the clerk juggling bright-colored balls.

Randy's hand dropped to his weapon, but Frank spread his hands away from his leathered Remington, palms forward. Randy rested his hand on the bar and Frank hooked a heel on the brass rail next to him. He nodded at the bartender, who realized he was still holding the bottle and cork and filled a fresh glass.

"How many's that?" Frank asked, tilting his head toward Randy's and meeting his gaze in the mirror mounted on the backbar.

"My second. I stop at two now, just enough to take the sting out of my leg."

"I do regret that. That horse you had throwed up its head or I'd of just kilt you instead of making you lame."

"Well, I taken your ear. I know how much store you set in good looks."

"It slowed me down some at the start, but since I got famous I ain't wanted for companionship."

"What about that woman you stole from her sheriff daddy in Colorado?"

"I left her and she died. That's another regret. Whenever I think of you I clean lose my good manners. As I recall, you always had a way in that department. I seen the most looksome women with the ugliest toads."

"They come, but they never stick. They expect you to put 'em first, leastwise when you're together. If it's another woman they can always scratch her face and pull out her hair, but they can't fight what they can't see. I never could commit to one like I do you."

"You might send flowers now and again, seeing as how you're so sweet on me."

"Go to hell, Frank."

"You first."

The tall deputy came in the door, his hand resting on his gun handle. His partner, the half-breed, stood on the threshold with his shotgun leveled. Frank and Randy turned to face them.

Randy said, "Gents, you better be as good as you think you are."

The tall deputy took in the two men with their hands hovering near their pistols. "How good you got to be with a street sweeper at your back?"

Frank said, "That's the trouble with a long narrow room like this. If he cuts loose, we all three go down squirting blood with all our inwards outside. So that makes two of us you got to take down all on your own."

The man with the paintbrush whiskers switched cheeks on his plug, switched back. He leaned over a little and shot a brown stream into the nearest spittoon. He caught his partner's eye in the mirror. The man with the shotgun backed out the door and turned away, followed by his partner, moving backwards also.

When they were alone with the bartender, mopping his face with his swamp rag, Frank said, "Can you get that pistol out of that soft holster in under two minutes?"

"If I hold the holster down with one hand and jerk hard."

"Me, too. We ought to ask Cripplehorn where he got

them slick holsters and tie-downs he writes about in his books. I reckon them boys are readers."

"Hell, I don't believe he ever wrote even one. Got time for a hand?"

Randy jerked down the rest of his drink. "Always."

They sat at one of the gaming tables while the bartender brought a deck of cards.

"I heard they grow their lawmen tough in the Strip," Cripplehorn said. "Is there no end to these myths?"

The half-breed Chickasaw cradled his shotgun. "We chose badly."

"I understand how you feel. You hear that?" The entrepreneur tilted his head in the direction of the tent. The band was still playing, but above the thumping brass and boom of the bass drum came the regular chugging beat of a freight train at full throttle. "They're pounding the bleachers with their feet. Before long they'll come streaming out screaming for their money back. The vendors have been plying them with beer all afternoon. I may be the first man ever strung up on a complaint of disappointment. What were they doing when you left?"

"I looked back in through the window," said the tall deputy. "They were playing cards."

"Locke and Farmer?"

"Yup."

"Playing cards."

"Yup."

"What kind of place is this, where men are shooting at each other one day and socializing the next?"

The half-breed rolled his shoulders. "If you spend enough time out here, you get used to everything."

"I've been crisscrossing the West for more than ten years. I'm not used to it yet."

"You just need more time."

Frank, who sat facing the window in the Rusty Bucket, shielded his eyes against the lowering sun. "Half-past two or thereabout. I forgot to wind my watch this morning; ain't used to wearing one after all them visits to pawnshops. Two cards." He laid down two.

Randy dealt him two off the deck. "That's what's good about the sun. It don't need winding."

"It's dependable, that's certain. Everybody knows when the sun'll come up and bed down; it's in the Almanac. But the moon comes and goes on its own and nobody knows when."

"That's on account of God made the sun, and He's an orderly man. The moon's the devil's work. Dealer takes one."

Both men raised the stake. The bartender came around with the bottle and a fresh glass for Randy, but Randy shook his head and Frank cupped his hand over his, preventing him from pouring. He returned to the bar and sat on a stool, dividing his attention between the *Fort Smith Elevator* and the Regulator clock clunking out the minutes on the wall opposite.

Frank asked Randy if he was thinking what Frank was.

"If I was, I wouldn't own to it."

"I'm thinking Cripplehorn's got no leave to poke around in what's between you and me, and nobody else neither."

Randy concentrated on his cards. "We gave him our word."

"Till day after tomorrow, we said. That's today."

"I never wanted this folderol to begin with," Randy said. "I only went along with it because I needed money at the time."

"Same here. It just feels like we're standing in downtown Denver in our long-handles with the flaps down. I don't figure he bought the right for that. Call."

Randy spread his cards on the green baize. "Two pair, jacks and deuces." The fifth card was the five of clubs.

Frank's teeth showed in his imperials. He laid his hand down faceup. He had two jacks and deuces and the five of hearts.

Randy said, "I've played poker all my life and watched a thousand games. I never saw such a thing before. I never even heard it could happen."

"That tears it, don't it?"

Randy looked up and smiled. "Who invited God into this game?"

TWENTY-FIVE

Nature is a random force, disaster its close cousin.

They selected the railroad tracks for the contest, Frank on the north side, Randy on the south. That placed the sun to Frank's left and Randy's right and at a disadvantage to neither man. No trains were scheduled before early evening. They took off their coats and laid them on the ground, Frank folding his carefully according to the creases, Randy letting his fall in a heap; that gave their arms freedom of movement. Randy, unaccustomed to his new hat, took it off and dropped it on top of the coat to avoid distraction.

The band music and the noise of hundreds of customers pounding the bleachers reached them from a distance, as of a storm on the other side of a mountain range, lightning pulsing and thunder a dull thud, dumping torrents, while they stood in the sun, utterly detached from someone else's tempest.

They squared off, raising their pistols to shoulder height

and extending them the length of their arms, hammers cocked.

"Drop your weapons or I'll shoot you both where you stand!"

The man who had stepped around the corner of the brick train station on Randy's side of the tracks was hatless, with his thick blue-black hair cut in a bowl and a bright star on his blue tunic. He held a Henry rifle braced against one shoulder, his other hand resting on the forepiece. He had features the color of brick, and with the sun carving caverns in his cheeks and the flat planes of his temples, seemingly as hard.

Frank and Randy faced off the way they played poker, allowing nothing to draw their eyes from the game.

"I'm an officer with the Cherokee Lighthorse Police and it's my intention to prevent murder on grounds entrusted to me. Drop 'em!" he roared.

Walter Red Hawk's reactions were slower than his sense of probity, and were no match for Randy's relentless practice or Frank's experience in the field. The Cherokee managed to fire only one shot before two pistol bullets struck him full in the chest. He went down, reflexively cranking a new round into the chamber, which was still in it unfired when he fell into the gravel off the edge of the station platform. His slug had passed between the two men as they wheeled his direction. The coroner's inquest the next day established death as instantaneous. Two rounds were dug out of the corpse, both of which had hit vital spots.

That event, taking place as it did in the more cramped venue of the Evangelical Church, was packed as closely as Cripplehorn's tent, with all the pews taken and spectators standing three deep in back. The dead man was known to most who attended, and popular. He'd supplemented his stipend from the tribal council working in the local sawmill and supported a Cherokee wife and two small children.

As the town had no jail, Randy and Frank were placed in custody in a room on the second floor of the hotel. The shots had drawn a crowd from the tent, who grasped the situation immediately and seized and disarmed them both; there were just too many of them to shoot and make an escape, so they held off. The city marshal, his deputies, and Walter Red Hawk's colleagues in the Lighthorse Police guarded the men in shifts while shouts reached them from the Rusty Bucket, which was the place of choice whenever informal hanging required discussion.

"They swung Spanish Bob in the church bell tower a couple of years back," the marshal informed his prisoners. "I'm not just sure any of those Cherokees with badges would place themselves between you two and a lynch mob with practical experience."

The peace officer's name was Foster. He wore a gray suit and town shoes and his hair was prematurely white. Strangers mistook him for a banker until they got close enough to study his brown seamed face and empty eyes. He carried a Schofield revolver on his belt and a squat English

Bulldog in a Wes Hardin rig under his left shoulder. In five years, the first two as a deputy, he'd shot eleven men and been acquitted of murder in one case where the evidence was doubtful.

Frank, who like Randy was stiff-limbed and swollen-faced from mishandling by the crowd, asked Foster what had become of Cripplehorn.

"He ran off with his cash box when the shooting started. I and my men were too busy keeping the pair of you from your appointment in church to look for him, and the Indian police didn't care. My thinking is he hid somewhere out in the trees till the eastbound came along and hooked it after it pulled out. Personally I don't give snake shit. If folks are dumb enough to shell out three days' wages to see two men try to kill each other when they can see it for free anywhere in the territory, it isn't my responsibility."

"What's to be done with us?" Randy asked.

"Assuming you survive the night we're putting you on the train to Fort Smith in the morning. I and my deputies will ride with you as far as Buffalo, over in the Cherokee Nation, where we'll hand you off to the federals. They'll see you the rest of the way." Foster stood with one foot on a stool upholstered in petit-point embroidered fabric and one arm resting on his thigh, watching them with his empty eyes. "If I were you I wouldn't mess with Parker's marshals. Half of them had shinplasters out on them before they signed on and the other half is just plain ornery. They don't want to shoot you, because then they'll have to pay for the burial out of their own pockets, but that won't slow them down if they find you're not worth the trouble of delivery. I'd wouldn't count on them being as easygoing as Walter Red Hawk. I've ridden with them and I know."

It was a long night in their lives, with voices murmuring down in the street and the flicker of torches through the window throwing crawling shadows on the ceiling. The half-breed with the shotgun was posted in their room, the orange point of his cigarette moving now and again and glowing more fiercely when he drew on it from his chair in the corner with a view of the window. His tall partner sat outside the door with a chair borrowed from another room and the back tilted and propped under the knob, where anyone would have to go through him to get in.

Randy said to the breed, "Just be sure that street sweeper ain't pointed too general when the ball starts."

"Shut up."

Frank lay for a while in silence, stretched out on the bed with his hands behind his head, watching the muted fireworks. One of his ankles was shackled to the bed's iron frame. "Where do folks get so many torches, I wonder, and so fast? You reckon this is such a normal thing they keep 'em in a nice dry place, pitched and ready?"

The guard told him to shut up too.

"Damnedest place I ever did see," said Randy, seated on the edge of the mattress with his feet on the floor, one of them chained like Frank's to his side of the bed. "They got law, but it don't raise a finger to stop the show, only when we took it outside. You reckon Cripplehorn had a license and didn't tell us about it?"

After another little stretch of quiet, the breed spoke. "Walter had it in his mind to stop you in the tent the minute you faced off. He was on his way there when he spotted you two trying to spoil everybody's day."

"How you know that?" Randy asked.

"Hell, he talked about it for weeks. I don't reckon anybody thought he'd act on it. Them Cherokees like to hear their tongues rattle like a gourd. This is the first time one actually done what he said he would."

"He should of kept his voice down," Frank said. "You don't shout at two men with guns when all you got is one."

Randy said, "I like a nice polite arrest. I don't mind if it involves me waking up with a knot on my head from some hoglegs swung by somebody knows how to swing it. I sure don't like to be squawked at like I'm married to a she-bear."

"Go to sleep, Randy. That'd have to be one desperate she-bear."

The half-Chickasaw deputy told them both to shut up.

TWENTY-SIX

Justice is man's invention. The universe makes no such promise.

A sudden downpour, not uncommon in November in that region, doused the dudgeon of the mob, which broke up into individuals sprinting for cover. Although it had re-formed the next day at the train station, the presence of Marshal Foster, all four of his deputies, and as many Light-horse Police, every man carrying a shotgun, kept things benign.

Frank and Randy were seated in facing seats, each shackled to a deputy. A fresh, green horse apple splatted against a window and the train began its journey through that feral country, where rocks pushed up like yellow-brown knuckles through the soil and half-naked trees clawed holes in the overcast.

In Fort Smith, Arkansas, where Judge Isaac Parker exercised federal jurisdiction over the Nations, the prosecutor and the attorney appointed to defend the prisoners debated whether the defendants should be tried separately (Parker overruled this), whether Walter Red Hawk had overstepped himself in attempting to arrest non-Indians (Parker allowed this argument to proceed), and whether two men can both be charged with the same homicide.

The celebrated "Hanging Judge" (twenty-five men convicted by that January of 1883, twenty-four hanged, one escaped) was intrigued by this argument. He'd presided over the court for seven years, and although the burden of his docket and awesome responsibility had streaked his hair and beard with white at age forty-four, a novel suggestion always brought him upright in his chair.

A partial transcript of the discussion between prosecutor Clayton, defense attorney MacElroy, and Judge Parker follows:

CLAYTON: Your honor, the coroner's inquest found both wounds fatal.

MACELROY: I submit, your honor, that whereas one bullet pierced the deceased's heart and the other punctured a lung, the first would have caused death immediately.

PARKER: Counselor, are you suggesting that one of your clients is more guilty than the other?

MACELROY: That would be unethical. I'm attempting to establish grounds for separate trials.

PARKER: I've already ruled on that. In any case, this court has no way of determining who fired which bullet. They come identical from the factory and are unrecognizable upon impact.

MACELROY: Your honor—

PARKER: Pursue another line, Counselor.

Whenever the trial recessed, Frank and Randy were returned, each man's wrists and ankles chained together, to their cells in the brick jail, which was built around a three-tiered steel cage, the latest in penal design with a gear-driven mechanism that allowed the guards to open or shut an entire line of cells just by throwing a lever. This made a hellish clang that had been known to break a man. The two men occupied different levels, with no way of communicating short of shouting, and the guards discouraged such breeches of the peace.

The remaining bone of contention—keenly observed by the reporters assigned from across the continent to cover the trial—was whether Walter Red Hawk, in interceding in an affair between white men, had exceeded his jurisdiction, which was confined to Indians by federal law. In his instructions to the jury, Parker left no question regarding his opinion on the matter: Notwithstanding the deceased's error in judgment, the willful slaying of a tribal officer and a ward of the U.S. government was a federal offense. After deliberating two hours, the panel of twelve returned a verdict of guilty. The defendants were sentenced to hang.

"Frankly, I wish it were from someone else's gallows,"

said Parker, raising his gavel. "We grow murderers enough here at home without importing more."

But the world wouldn't quit turning.

Things had changed since the days when Parker suffered no interference from Washington. In the early years of his tenure, no appeal existed between him and the president—or God Almighty, some said, because showing mercy to murderers cost votes, particularly in the wild territories; but the Judge had enemies in the Congress. They argued that no man's influence was greater than both houses combined, and pushed through a bill placing the infamous Eleventh District firmly in the appeals system that applied to other courts.

The eastern newspapers applauded the decision, while privately regretting the loss of sensational accounts of wholesale executions on the great Fort Smith scaffold. Such headlines as SIX MEN "JERKED TO JESUS" IN A HEARTBEAT did more for circulation than war with Canada.

And so those stalwart public servants Flapdoodle, Pettifog, and Straddler succeeded in gelding the old bull at last.

Seeing the advantage in publicity—for Abraham Cripplehorns are rather more common among attorneys than most other places—the lawyer who'd been appointed to represent Frank and Randy reopened their file. His name was F.S.T. MacElroy: "Feisty" to his fellow law students at

William and Mary, and he had earned the nickname through more than just his initials. Feisty hired a jeweler.

The jeweler, Otto Weismann, wore a skullcap and a loupe hinged to his wire spectacles. He used his scales to weigh the two bullets that had been removed from Walter Red Hawk's corpse, which the coroner in Cimarron had placed in separate envelopes labeled HEART and LUNG. The slugs were both intact, although misshapen by passage through the flesh. The difference in weight was almost infinitesimal, but inarguable: The bullet that had penetrated the left lung—a long, agonizing death when left on its own—was a .45. The other, which had stopped the heart upon contact, causing instant death, was a .44. Weismann signed an affidavit swearing to his conclusions and it was sent to the court of appeals.

The newspapers reported the event, to keep alive a story they'd missed covering, but overlooking its significance: It was the birth of modern ballistic science.

Frank Farmer had reason to be thankful he'd replaced his lost .44 New Model Remington revolver with a .45, cracked grips or no. That tiny difference in calibers spared him the gallows.

Armed with this information, F.S.T. MacElroy wrote to Chester Alan Arthur, who at the time was stinging from public accusations about his wardheeling past and needed a reputation as a progressive. He commuted Frank's sentence to life.

But the lawyer wasn't done. He filed a petition asking

for a second trial for his clients based on his earlier argument that the slain peace officer had lacked the authority to arrest them. The petition was granted, but for unexplained reasons only Randy's conviction was set aside. The attorney's protests were ignored. Bail was denied. Randy languished in his cell until April 1885, when a new jury heard his case. Once again, Parker presided. His hair and whiskers now were nearly all white.

"Mr. Blood, did you say in the presence of the defendant that you tried to talk Walter Red Hawk out of attempting to restrain Frank Farmer and Randolph Locke from shooting each other?" asked lawyer MacElroy.

"No." Deputy Marshal Billy Blood, the half-Chickasaw from Cimarron, sat in the witness chair with his feet flat on the floor and his plate star shining on his blue tunic. "What I said was I didn't believe him when he said he would."

"Objection."

"On what grounds, Mr. Clayton?" Parker asked the prosecutor.

"Leading the witness."

"Sustained."

"I'll rephrase the question. Why didn't you believe him, Mr. Blood?"

"Cherokees are all talk and no action. Everybody knows that."

"Objection! Conclusion on the part of the witness."

"Sustained. Mr. Blood, old antagonisms between the tribes are of no interest to this court."

The defense attorney repeated the question. Billy Blood fidgeted, then said:

"Walter always went by the book, and the book says Indian officers can't touch white men. They're for U.S. marshals and deputized city policemen."

After the summations, Parker addressed the jury, reiterating what he'd said in the first trial about the killing of tribal officers and wards of the government.

Whether because his iron rule had been challenged by the Congress or for other reasons known only to the jurors, the Judge was less convincing this time. Three days of deliberation ended in deadlock. A mistrial was declared and Randy was returned to custody to await a third trial. In December of the same year he rose before the judge of the Third District Court in Fort Scott, Kansas, and learned he'd been acquitted on grounds of self-defense.

He was free, while Frank was removed to the Federal House of Corrections in Detroit, Michigan, to serve out the rest of his days at hard labor.

"That ain't fair," said Randy.

He was back in Fort Smith to claim his belongings, including the Ballard and the Colt, which had been removed from three years in evidence.

MacElroy, a son of the Commonwealth of Virginia who smoked cigarettes in a long onyx holder to avoid staining his fair Van Dyke beard, nodded. He'd invited his client to his office, a cramped room smelling of dust and rotted bindings overlooking Garrison Avenue, to give him the news. A heating stove intended for a much larger room made the air oppressive.

"It's worse than unfair; it's indifferent. The implication is Frank's case was closed when he was taken off Death Row."

"What you fixing to do about it?"

"Oh, I'll write letters."

"That's it?"

"It was sufficient to save you both from execution. I might wear them down. You never know. I have a reputation for perseverance."

"That son of a bitch Parker had us both measured for the rope. I still like him better than this bunch in Washington. You know he cried when he said we'd be hung by the neck till dead, him that'd said the same thing twenty-five times already?"

"He's a sentimental old ogre. Prays in the Methodist church for the souls of the men he sent to hell."

"I bet Chet Arthur never shed a tear when he buried Frank alive."

"Well, there's a new president. I doubt Cleveland would have granted my petition."

"He's the sixth since Frank and I been fighting."

"I expected you to be pleased. I've been through the transcripts of your double trial so many times I can recite them chapter and verse. I never read of a kind word passing between you."

"Just because you want a fellow dead don't mean you want him locked up in Michigan."

"I'm afraid your gentleman-duellist's ideas of honor don't apply to the criminal justice system."

"It's criminal all right."

TWENTY-SEVEN

Time is worse than a thief. It murders youth and hope.

Fifteen years plodded past, pulled by oxen. At times they seemed to stop utterly, caught in mire or forced to wait for water to recede. The pace was the same for both men, outside as well as in.

The world spun around them. It was like being stuck trackside with a busted wheel, watching trains hurtle past, all the faces in the windows a blur.

Geronimo, a great butcher and liar to his people, surrendered himself and his band of thirty Chiricahua to General Miles in a place called Skeleton Canyon, turning himself from a bloodthirsty savage to a celebrity overnight.

Another fierce winter, worse than the one that had closed the Lazy Y and most of its competitors in 1882, swept away the last of the open range, leaving behind fenced ranches, truck farms, and hundreds of tons of bloated cattle carcasses to be buried in mass graves.

The *San Francisco Examiner* ran out of gunfights and published a poem by Ernest Lawrence Thayer called "Casey at the Bat."

The Indian Nations, now known as Oklahoma Territory, hosted a barn-burner of a horse race: Hundreds of would-be homesteaders whipping teams and mounts into a lather to claim 160 acres apiece in free land. The Cherokee Strip vanished overnight, its original settlers pushed aside and the scum of the earth fled to Canada and Mexico.

The Congress and President Benjamin Harrison sliced Dakota in two, bunched it in with Montana, Washington, Idaho, and Wyoming to bring the total of U.S. states to forty-four.

A gang of Oklahoma stick-up artists experimented with bank robbery in Kansas, and got themselves shot to ribbons for stepping outside their specialty, which was robbing trains. Four men paid for it with their lives, including two brothers named Dalton.

The first copies of *The National Geographic* found their way into barbershops, where the African issues wore out faster than the edge on a razor.

A nobody named Selman shot John Wesley Hardin to death in El Paso, prudently from behind.

A battleship went down off Cuba and that fool McKinley declared war on the whole goldarn Spanish Empire.

Meanwhile, Frank slept nights in an eight-by-five cell in Detroit and busted rocks days to pave the streets for automobiles, and Randy tried suicide.

It's difficult to say which man suffered more: Frank, because of the unremitting hardship and monotony of incarceration, or Randy, because the purpose of his existence—to end Frank's—had been stolen from him with the flick of a little wooden mallet.

In Sedalia, Missouri, he aimed his Colt at his temple, but owing to his drunken condition missed and shot off the end of his nose, resulting in copious bleeding but not death. The woman who ran the boarding house found him, and charged him for the ruined bedding after the bandages came off.

Suicide was against state law, although no one who'd succeeded had ever been prosecuted. Instead of jailing him, the city police put him in a lock ward at the hospital and strapped him to a bed. When after three days he promised a foreigner in a white coat with a billy-goat beard he wouldn't repeat the offense, he was released and his weapon returned to him. He'd sold the Ballard for grocery money a year earlier, the West being wolfed out and Randy so far outside rifle range. He kept the pistol to shoot rats and such, his usual accommodations not measuring up to the standards of the Eldorado.

One night, lying wide awake amongst the vermin in a five-cent-a-room palace in Jefferson City, his Colt out to protect his boots from the men snoring in the surrounding beds, he got a brainstorm from a pint bottle: Everybody was always trying to break out of prison, but nobody ever tried to break in. They wouldn't be expecting that.

Hopping trains wasn't as easy as it was once. The new coal-burners were greased lightning, and with the country going through one of its panics all the guards were on the prod for tramps. After several false tries he managed to grab a handle on a westbound, and to jump off when the train slowed for a curve outside Pawnee, O.T. There he walked into a hardware store run by a husband and wife from Wisconsin, place cluttered with rolls of barbed and baling wire, hickory axe handles, and Sears, Roebuck catalogues, shot a hole in a nail keg, and demanded cash. But the husband was unfamiliar with the new cash register, brass and bronze and big as a plow, and terrified besides. Randy was watching him fumble for the magic combination of keys and crank that would open the drawer when the wife crept up behind the desperado and swung an axe handle at his head, putting a crack in it and ruining his Texas hat.

In the Fort Smith courtroom, he fingered the lump where his head had been shaved, stitched, and plastered and waited for Parker to come in, adjudicate, and ship him off to Detroit. Once he was in the House of Corrections, he reckoned, any sort of makeshift weapon would save the nation the expense of boarding Frank Farmer for the remainder of his natural span.

But he hadn't read a newspaper in months and didn't know that Judge Parker had died in office after twenty-one years on the bench. The squirt who showed up looked like a little kid in the big horsehair chair behind the massive cherrywood desk. He gave Randy three to five years in the federal penitentiary at Little Rock, four hundred miles from his target.

Meanwhile, a letter arrived at a cramped overheated office overlooking Garrison Avenue in Fort Smith:

Office of the Attorney General
Washington, D.C.

Dear F.S.T. MacElroy, esq.:

In response to your letters regarding Francis X. Farmer, please be advised that this office is considering your request for a hearing to determine whether parole is indicated. . . .

The honest Indians of Oklahoma Territory mourned Isaac Parker, who had brought swift justice so many times on their behalf. Not so the Congress. Its members picked over his carcass, divvied up what was left of his jurisdiction, and reviewed all his decisions starting with when Hector was a pup. Some were let stand, others reversed and the prisoners granted either new trials or a presidential pardon. Still others were paroled. On June 5, 1900, Frank Farmer walked into a mostly empty room where five men sat behind a long table from a Masonic lodge and walked out a free man.

The news got five lines from editors who vaguely recalled the drama of Locke *vs.* Farmer. The *Barbary Spar,* owned and operated still by Major W.B. Updegraff, bald now and stone deaf, made use of improved photograph reproduction and accompanied the piece with the picture taken of Randy and Frank in Cimarron, cropped to the size of a postage stamp. The one-column headline read:

FRONTIER ERA GUNMAN RELEASED.

Newspapers were banned in the Little Rock penitentiary, to avoid exciting the inmates with stories of crime and pictures of Russian ballerinas in tights; but if you had the contacts and had put back a little money you could get anything. Randy hadn't had much to put back, but what he scrimped on tobacco makings he saved for news from the outside world. With things moving so fast all around, you never knew when the status quo might make a square turn.

His stomach sank when he found the teeny piece about Frank in the telegraph column of the *Little Rock Gazette.* Luck and timing had been against him so long he reckoned the Lord had it in for him for all those times he'd taken His name in vain. But then his heart quickened. If he behaved himself, he, too, would be out in eighteen months; no time at all when you stood it up against twenty-five years.

TWENTY-EIGHT

An ocean voyage is the best remedy for the stagnant soul.

Frank Farmer thought San Francisco the biggest, fastest, loudest place in the world: the boldest whores, the busiest streets, saloons the size of cotton warehouses.

Then he saw Nome.

It was a sprawl bigger than Creede or Deadwood in their time. The beach was a sea of tents, enough canvas to make a thousand as big as Cripplehorn's show tent outside Cimarron. With nothing to separate them but duck stretched over frame, the tin-tack pianos, banjos, and string bands made a racket like a trainload of kettles tumbling down a ravine. The place had more whorehouses than Dodge City, Denver, and Tombstone combined, some of them honest-to-God cribs where a hostess entertained you in the little wooden rick where she slept, stacked one on top of the next in rows like crates in a warehouse, and you could track the progress of what was going on in each house from ten doors down. There was no escape from the bustle except the hop joints, where a man could crawl into a bunk and smoke up unobtainable women and colors that didn't exist.

Someone had stubbed his toe on a nugget in Alaska, and the rest of the world came running.

Back in Frisco, where the ships set sail, you couldn't cross a street without taking the chance of being run over by a carriage or a buckboard or a by-God automobile, squawking its horn and choking on its own exhaust with a bang that throwed your heart into your throat, thinking you'd been dry-gulched. You could walk across the harbor, stepping from schooner to steamship to tugboat to barge and never get your feet wet. It might've been that way clear to Alaska, but it wasn't. Frank bought a berth on a steamer called the *Pelican,* and found himself on the ocean for the first time in his life.

If Randy was alive—and he was sure he'd know if he wasn't—Nome was where he'd be found.

Neither man could resist going someplace where people gathered in herds. It was the best place to look. Big mining interests had claimed the gold fields of California and Colorado from under the feet of individual fortune-seekers, the silver mines had played out or flooded, and for all the annoyance they brought with them the ticking of horseless carriages was still too faint to excite much interest in the vast pools of oil slumbering beneath Texas and Pennsylvania. Best of all, Nome had few laws and fewer men still to enforce them. It was like the old Cherokee Strip without that pest Cripplehorn to spoil things.

It was a rough crossing. The sea stood up on its hind legs and pitched over onto its forefeet, arching and twisting, sunfishing like an unbroke mustang by Beelzebub out of a waterspout. Frank got right well acquainted with the lee rail of the *Pelican* and decided if Randy didn't get lucky and kill him he'd find his way back home on foot somehow.

His first day outside, Randy broke another law.

He spent the wages he'd made working the mangle in the prison laundry on a day coach and crossed the state line four hours later, violating the terms of his parole.

"Where you off to, old-timer?" asked the man in the seat facing his, a fellow in a striped coat and straw boater who looked like one-fourth of a barbershop quartet.

"North."

"You caught the wrong train. This one's heading west."

"It was the first one out of the station."

"What's your hurry?"

He allowed himself a bitter grin. "Gonna get rich up in Alaska."

It was a long way, a man had to eat, and the jobs didn't come in a straight line. He loaded bales of cotton and barrels of molasses aboard flatboats in New Orleans, spread tar on the streets of Houston, cleaned and polished cuspidors and swamped up vomit in a saloon called La Perla in the Spanish peninsula of Baja, California. The Mexican government appeared to have lost interest in banishing him from the republic. He slept in barns and stables and out in the open. He was a ghost, a figure of derision in rags with a short nose. He spent a night in jail in Yuba City for jerking his pistol on a gang of boys who pelted him with gravel and horse apples.

Randy hated boats and such truck; losing his horse and gear when that ferry capsized by Fort Benton in '77 was as close to a sailing man as he ever cared to get. But unless they built a bridge, he knew he'd have to put up with some ocean. There was too much of it between Frisco and Nome, so he set his sights on Seattle.

He got as far as Puyallup, collapsed in the street, and lay there two hours before someone noticed and took him to a hospital for the indigent with as bad a case of pneumonia as had ever been admitted there. A month later, still weak but turned out because his bed was needed, he rode with a pile of fish to Seattle, where he put in for cook's helper aboard a sealer bound for the Bering Sea.

The captain was clerkly looking, with graying burnsides. He sat with his tunic buttoned to his neck at a table in a room stacked with sacks and barrels and smelling of the sea.

"Before you sign, understand we're not putting in at

Nome. I've had trouble with gold fever and desertions. If you try going over the side, I'll invoke maritime law and have you shot."

Randy signed.

The cook had about the same talent as his helper, although he made better biscuits. Randy labored visibly climbing to the captain's cabin carrying dishes on trays, stopped frequently in passageways to lean against a bulkhead to catch his breath, sweated buckets. By the time the ship passed the Aleutians, its master and crew were no longer paying him any attention, except to wonder if they'd have a corpse to send over the side.

"He's a curious cuss, that's certain," said the first mate. "Always asking landlubbers' questions and watching how we do things."

The captain frowned. "Ordinarily I'd tell Cookie to give him something useful to do with all that spare time; but he's one played-out fish. Serves me right for taking pity on an old man with only a bedroll to his name. I wasted a lecture."

They were creeping along the territory's northwest coast, the man in the crow's nest watching for ice floes, when the bosun pointed the stem of his pipe at a glitter in the otherwise solid black off starboard. "Nome."

Randy waited until the man went below, then swept the canvas sheet off a lifeboat stored with supplies and provisions pilfered from the galley and sea chest, climbed in, and lowered himself by pulleys to the water.

It was a hellish voyage: What the crew considered a calm sea was to him a tempest, he was clumsy with the oars, and the scudding fog obscured the lights ashore for minutes at a time, during which he was certain he'd come around and was rowing away from land. That terrified him more than being shot to death; more than prison. A Texas cowboy had no business drowning in a frozen sea.

When at last the incoming tide took over, drawing the boat into the shallows, he couldn't wait for it to ground. He bundled his foodstuffs and personals in an oilcloth slicker, got out, and waded.

Once on the beach, pale in the light from the settlement, the wire broke that had been holding him together. He dropped his bundle and followed it down to the ground.

Lying on his back chasing his breath, he saw a ragged sliver of moon through a tear in the clouds.

Everybody knows when the sun'll come up and bed down; it's in the Almanac. But the moon comes and goes on its own and nobody knows when.

That's on account of God made the sun, and He's an orderly man. The moon's the devil's work.

"Well, Frank," he whispered, "I shoveled puke, scoured grease, spit up blood, and crossed a goddamn ocean. If you ain't here, I'll track you down and kill you twice."

TWENTY-NINE

Upon encountering an old friend after a separation of years,
resist the urge to remark upon how much he's aged.
The chances are he's thinking the same thing about you.

The gaunt, moustachioed barkeep of the Broadway Saloon sighed when he recognized Frank shoving his way through the crowd to the bar.

"No, mister," he said, "I ain't seen no mangy piece of wolf bait today. Leastwise not one answering to Randy Locke."

"Who the hell was that?" asked a prospector drinking a beer, jerking his head toward the departing man.

"I forgot his name the minute he give it. Been in every day for a month asking the same question."

Frank worked all the way down Front Street, asking the same question in the Dexter, the Cosmopolitan, the Acme, and all the rest; identical, every one, hung with moose heads and snowshoes and smelling pungently of unwashed wool steaming in the heat of a cookstove. He got the same answer, as he had every day since he'd arrived in Nome.

There was no reason to leave a description of the man he was looking for. Neither man had ever shied from leaving his true name, and in all candor any description he might give would fit half that population of frostbitten prospectors caked with blue clay to their boot-tops, even if it was any good after fifteen years. When Randy did show up, he'd make the same rounds Frank had, asking after him.

The next day he started in fresh, not even having to ask the question now and leaving without a word after the answer. In the Parisian he was already turning away when he realized he'd hit paydirt.

"I ain't just certain," said the barman. "He was drunk and mumbled the name. I locked him up in the storeroom to keep him from getting his throat cut for what was in his pockets."

"Mighty big of you."

"I'm a Christian, mister."

Frank watched him unlock the door to the room behind the bar and followed him through. Randy lay spread-eagled among the barrels and crates, snoring loud enough to rattle the empty bottles awaiting refilling on the shelves.

"He's high-smelling. I'd be obliged if you'd take him on out of here."

Frank sent him away with a cartwheel dollar and hauled Randy to his feet by one arm. An empty bottle of Old Pepper slid to the floor and rolled to a stop against a rat trap, springing it with a loud snap.

In the New York Kitchen Frank half-dragged, half-carried him to an oilcloth-covered table and dumped him into a chair. Two men seated at a nearby table picked up their plates and moved to the other side of the room.

A waiter with a full beard and a white apron that hung to his knees appeared.

"We don't serve tramps. You want to buy him a bowl of soup, you send him around back."

The muzzle of a Remington revolver planted itself against the waiter's forehead.

"Mister, you got two choices."

"What'll it be?"

Frank lowered the hammer and holstered the pistol. "Coffee. Bring the pot."

When it came, Frank filled a thick china mug, pulled Randy's head up from the table by his hair, and poured coffee into his open mouth. He choked, sputtered, shook loose of the other's grip, and slapped at his hip. Frank slapped him harder across the face and went on slapping until Randy's eyes came into focus.

"You son of a bitch!"

"That's what my daddy said." He sat down, filled the mug again, pushed it across the table, and watched him raise it to his lips with both hands. They shook. His shirt was full of holes and he smelled as if he'd rolled in a puddle of rancid grease. "You keep on with that skullbender you'll cheat me out of what I got coming."

"It's the only thing here that's cheap."

"They stir it up on the spot and refill the bottles. You can buy two for the price of an egg. When'd you get in?"

"Last night late; waded in. I had to thaw out. This place is colder than the winter of '81."

"They say it gets worse come November." Frank pushed some banknotes across the table. "Finish that pot and buy yourself some decent clothes. I can't shoot you in this condition."

"Struck it rich?"

"It'd surprise you how much money you can make busting rocks fifteen years. I didn't spend none of it inside and I'm camped out on the beach. You can look for me there when you stop shaking."

Frank was almost at the door when a hammer cocked behind him. He spun, clapping his holster with one hand and snatching out the Remington with the other, just in time to see Randy's Colt blow a hole in the waiter's apron. The man was still holding his sawed-off shotgun when he hit the floor.

When Randy laid the pistol on the table, Frank leathered his. "Obliged."

Randy lifted his cup, steadily now with one hand.

"I didn't spare you nothing you ain't got coming."

Frank was dousing his nerves in the Broadway when a miner came in wearing muddy overalls. "Your name Farmer?"

"Who's asking?"

"You better come get your friend. He's over at the Sitka, drinking out the joint and calling all the customers every kind of a son of a bitch. They're fixing to bust him to pieces."

The Sitka stood at the end of Front Street with an eight-foot totem pole beside the entrance. Frank ran inside, just behind the Remington. From old habit he ducked the big tin hurricane lamp that hung too far down from the low ceiling, but failed to duck the hard object that struck him from behind.

When he came to himself, wrists and ankles bound and slung facedown across a pack saddle, he knew himself for a fool. The leader of a party of fur-clad locals who dumped him into a snowdrift north of town explained to him that he had been posted out of town under the laws of the State of Oregon for disturbing the public peace.

"This ain't Oregon." Cut loose, Frank sat up, packed a snowball, and pressed it against the tender spot on the back of his head. His rubber ear was missing.

"Alaska's governed by Oregon law," said the man, built bearish with icicles in his beard. "By order of the Organic Act of 1884. We're special deputies sworn to uphold it."

"What peace did I disturb?"

"We don't like our waiters getting shot."

"I didn't shoot him. Anyway, he was fixing to bushwhack me when Randy gunned him."

"He's dead on account of you, and since he is, we can't post him out of town. Anyway, Nome needs waiters more'n it needs gun men. We're running out of rope."

"How's Randy? Last I heard he was about to get whupped by half of Nome."

"That was a story to smoke you out of the Broadway. The bunch that hangs out there disagree with the Organic Act of 1884."

"What drift you throw him in?"

"None. We pulled him out of the New York Kitchen and put him on the last boat headed to the States till spring."

"Where do I go till then?"

The man said something in a language Frank had never heard before to a man with features the color and apparent texture of iron. The man said something back, pointing into the teeth of the stinging wind.

"There's a party of Eskimo hunters camped a couple miles due north," the icicle man said. "I was you, I'd get there before sundown. We got wolves make the ones down south look like squirrels. That's why we let you keep your iron. Good luck with grizzlies. You don't want to know how big we grow *them*."

He took it out carefully, saw that the chambers were empty. "I don't reckon you know what become of my ear."

"That what that was? I stepped on it without knowing

and it broke. I thought it was a small king crab got away from the New York Kitchen."

"It got brittle. No hard feelings, Sheriff."

"I ain't a sheriff. Sheriff's back in Portland. I'm a special deputy, and if you try coming back to Nome, I'll make it my special responsibility to shoot you on sight. There will be hard feelings then."

It was an Aleut camp, actually.

By day the men, their faces pierced and plugged with ivory ornaments, walked miles out onto the icepack to shoot seals with their bows while their women tended the cook fires and mended and made warm coats from the skins of their prey. By night they slept in skin huts with snow plastered on the outside to keep out the cold. Their chief, who had been baptized into the Russian Orthodox Church, wore a crucifix carved from ivory on a sinew thong around his neck and smoked tobacco through a ptarmigan-bone pipe with an ivory bowl. He had no English, but was eloquent in sign.

Frank spent the winter, skinning and doing chores for his keep. He traded his extra cartridges for a coat and the fur boots they called mukluks. The women pried loose the bullets and mixed the powder with water for ink to tattoo their chins. Sometimes, when gales raged, howling like the icicle man's giant wolves and slinging razors of ice, the seal-oil lamps made it so hot in the huts Frank slept naked and sweating.

He saw one of the icicle man's gargantuan grizzlies at a distance, playfully batting around a walrus that bellowed and died and the bear ate it. He calculated it stood twelve feet high on its hind legs. However, he was under the influence of a native remedy made from otter piss filtered through fermented trade grain, and distrusted the sight. Alaska was so far out on the frontier it was almost civilization.

Frank didn't begrudge the time lost. He'd been snowed in before, and prison taught a man patience or it broke him. Come what would of the frontier, there would always be strikes and industry, and towns grown up around them overnight. He'd find Randy in one.

He just didn't know it would take as long as it did.

THIRTY

Opportunity is a cat, not a dog. It won't come to you; you must go out and bring it back.

The calendar shed leaves like buffalo hair, singly at first, then in clumps. Buckboards receded from the road, nudged aside by Model T trucks. Mercantiles became markets, filling orders placed by telephone. Electrified streets glowed bright as day in the dead of night. A Johnny Reb named D. W. Griffith moved into the vacancy left by P. T. Barnum, a good Yankee. It seemed the only place you saw an Indian was on a billboard selling chewing tobacco. In Dodge City, they tore down the Lady Gay Dance Hall and put up a roller-skating rink in its place.

When the first gusher came in at a place called Beaumont, Texas, Frank Farmer took a job protecting wildcat oil wells from slant drillers, driving away anyone attempting to build a derrick within twenty-five yards of his employers' with volleys from his Winchester. He asked around for Randy—a big chore in a town that had grown from nine thousand to fifty thousand souls in two years—but he never showed. He couldn't know that his old adversary was stuck in Glenn Pool, Oklahoma Territory, recovering from eight broken ribs on Indian land suddenly no longer worthless; before that he'd worked as a cook for the West Virginia Oil Company, and spent his time off asking for Frank. He'd decided to pack it in and try his luck in Beaumont when a block-and-tackle failed and dropped ten feet of pipe on him. That was in 1905.

In 1909, after performing much the same duties with his Winchester, Frank got a job helping to transport portable jail cells to overnight boomtowns that lacked such facilities on a permanent basis. The cells were made from iron strips riveted together and looked like big chicken coops when they were loaded aboard the wagon. Communities paid top dollar for the cages, so the wages were good and it was easy work; the recipients were so eager to accept shipment they did the unloading themselves. At every stop, Frank bent over the faces of drunks chained to trees while they sobered up, but none belonged to Randy.

When Randy, making some of the same stops, got into a fight with a drunken Osage oil millionaire in Cushing Field, O.T., he spent a night in one of Frank's portable cells, but couldn't sleep for restlessness. He was unsure why.

Frank tried speculating on his own in 1912. He reckoned that if dry places like Texas and Oklahoma gave up oil, so would Nevada, where he'd be the first to try his luck.

He borrowed money from a banker who was impressed with the well-dressed middle-aged man who wore his hair over his ears and tied into a little queue in back, bought equipment, and freighted it to Carson City in a wagon.

He was checking into the Empress Catherine Hotel when a signature farther up the page caught his eye. He hooked on a pair of spectacles and read Randy's name in a big round hand. His own hand shook when he tapped the name with his spectacles. "What room's Locke in?"

The clerk slid his own spectacles down his nose to read upside down, then poked them back onto the bridge. "He checked out night before last."

"Say where he was headed?"

"He said to tell anyone who asked to look for him in Californy. That's how he said it, with a *y*. Your friend isn't very well educated."

"He's ignorant as a drift fence, and he ain't my friend. I'm checking out." He picked up the pen again and drew a line through his name.

"California's a big place, mister. How do you expect to find him?"

"In a big crowd."

Frank unhitched a horse from his team and wired the banker to tell him where he could find his equipment. The banker hired the Pinkerton National Detective Agency to find him and arrest him for fraud, but when other speculators went bust looking for oil in Nevada, he considered himself fortunate things turned out as they had. He called off the investigation.

Understand, much of this is guesswork on my part. I got some of the story from Frank in Los Angeles where we were both working for the studios, some from cowboys and wranglers employed by them also who had worked ranches with them after they left the Circle X, and filled in the rest from imagination leavened by personal experience. I don't pretend that this is a true account; but I challenge anyone else to do better.

Frank was friendly and liked to talk about himself. He was too old to wrangle or herd, but he was kept busy working as an extra in what they called outdoor dramas. Directors liked his looks, with his Buffalo Bill whiskers and long silvering hair worn long to cover the hole where one ear was missing, and used him to dress up saloon sets and necktie parties; he looked good in his range clothes holding a flickering torch and was usually up front for Bill Hart or Tom Mix to shoot him first and dispel the mob.

I asked him why all the fuss with Randy. It was no surprise he had an answer ready.

"You ever try to drive a nail and it just won't go in straight? It's never the fault of the nail; there's a knot in the wood or you just ain't a good nailer. But you blame the nail anyway, just like it's a bad man or an ornery dog. You just plain hate it, and for no good reason.

"Well, sir, that there's Randy in a nutshell."

I never could get Randy to sit down and talk. He ignored me the first time, growled at me the second, and as I approached him for one more try he gathered up his cook's apron in one hand and rested the other on his Colt. He was an extra part-time—if you went to the pictures and saw an old man smoking a pipe and rocking on a front porch, it was him more than likely—and did some cooking for the cast and crew when a company went on location.

He was a disagreeable old cuss, and his enemy genial; but I liked Randy better. Frank was full of himself, and I suspect he pumped up his personal exploits considerable. I didn't dislike him so much as I thought he was a clumsy liar, laughing self-consciously at his own tall tales like a poker player who couldn't bluff. Randy didn't care what folks thought of him, which is an appealing trait. We might have been friends if Frank had never left Pennsylvania. Like any good hunter, Randy thought only of his prey.

I was going to write a scenario about their generation-long feud; I had a story editor at Triangle mildly interested in it as a possible vehicle for Mix and Carey. But I never did. There was no redemption in it to iris out on at the end.

Hollywood, California, was the last western boomtown. It had all the vices you expect of such places, but they got played up more in the newspapers because the people who practiced them had their faces plastered on full-color posters in neighborhood theaters across the country and grinned and snarled and wiggled their eyebrows on screens where their faces were blowed up twenty times life size. You saw them on the covers of magazines, read about what they slept in and how they ate and what kind of automobiles they drove, so when a matinee idol got arrested in a men-only brothel or a little sweetheart fell down a flight of stairs with a snootful of cocaine, the story drove President Taft clean off the front page.

There was killing, too; and long before those sordid cases involving fat actors and big-time directors.

Westerns were the moving pictures' most popular product. After the industry moved to California to take advantage of the light, it found all the mountains and deserts it needed to represent any territory in the old frontier without having to paint a single backdrop. And it struck paydirt in talent. When the last of the great ranches stopped hiring, all the boys gathered up their gear and headed to where the jobs were. They looked after the picturesque livestock for wages, sometimes wandered into a shot or were invited into one because of their look, and the outfit saved on wardrobe and equipment because they came with their own. A few of them even became stars. Will Rogers and Hoot Gibson went straight from scratchy bedrolls to silk sheets.

There was no lack for work. At a saloon called the Watering Hole in the heart of Los Angeles, a man with range experience could stand on the corner for a couple of hours and see everyone he knew, doing rope tricks and such to attract the attention of a passing casting director. A tenderheel from back East named Harry Carey hung around stealing authenticity.

I never could find the tracks in publishing after I left the Cody outfit. I think those marathon Indian fights and saving homesteaders' daughters from runaway horses ruined me for writing literature under my own name. I killed more men in a chapter than Crazy Horse at the Little Big Horn. When my money ran out in Dayton, Ohio, I left behind a trunkful of manuscripts and another trunkful of rejections and joined the westward migration. In no time at all I landed a spot polishing a scenario for Thomas Ince on his five-thousand-acre backlot north of Santa Monica—the place was rolling fat with actors and directors but thin on writers—and after *Custer's Last Fight* came in under budget and ahead of schedule I was offered a steady job. I accepted; the work was easy, and because no words were spoken on film, except on title cards when explanation was needed, a forty-four-minute two-reeler ran about ten pages. It paid better than working cattle and you could do it in your long-handles.

Biograph was paying better, though, so I quit and went there. But Griffith didn't like my writing—said it read like a Ned Buntline dime novel—and in less than a week I was through with the best outfit in the business. That's how

I came to be a fellow employee of Frank's and Randy's for the first time since 1868.

Neither man was interested in meeting featured players; *stars,* folks were calling them now, and the feeling was mutual on the stars' part.

The years since they got out of the oil business had not been kind to Frank and Randy. They'd been up and down, down more than up, which is where aging sets in. Frank kept his hat on inside and out because that long hair the directors found so photogenic lost its glamour when you saw his scalp poking up through it. Randy was getting bent, his leg dragged worse than always, and that patch of frost-bitten skin that hadn't patched itself up since buffalo days leaked into his scraggy beard. The sight of it put some off their feed, and so he drifted from one studio commissary to the next, still practicing making biscuits.

It was 1913. They'd been shooting at each other for forty-five years, longer than many friendships and most marriages. The death of either man—no matter if they were separated by a thousand miles of prairie or a city block—would be known for certain to the survivor the instant the spirit was divided from the body. So deep was their bond of hatred, the only consistent thing in their lives, and to which they were entirely faithful.

They had, in fact, been separated by considerably more than a thousand miles, and by something less than a city block. For a time, Frank Farmer had joined one of the lesser

Wild West exhibitions ("Arapaho Bob's Frontier Extravaganza and Confederation of Bordermen, Indian Princesses, and Savage Riders of the Plains! No Whitewash, No Hogwash, No Washing of Hands!"), shooting at blown-glass balls with his aging Winchester and not missing many, and toured with the troupe to England while Randy was driving an ice wagon in Bismarck. When Randy Locke lay near death from malaria in Panama City, contracted while digging the great canal, Frank, who'd been stranded abroad when the exhibition went bust, was working his way home by way of Nova Scotia, shoveling coal into the firebox of a tramp steamer.

Once, when Frank was chasing a rumor that Randy was laying a natural-gas pipeline in Wichita Falls, Randy was on his way to Amarillo, where Frank was said to be doing the same. Their trains passed only yards apart. (Each felt a chill on the instant.)

Fort Mescalero was shooting outside Palm Springs. The carpenters had gone and built a stake fort in what was supposed to be the Arizona desert, where everything was made of mud because the nearest tree was in Colorado; but then the Apaches all wore Cheyenne warbonnets and five minutes into the first reel the shadow of an aeroplane can be seen sliding across a wagon train. The director was known for never doing retakes and bringing productions in on time.

Frank was cast as an old mountain man to balance out the cigar-store Indian standing on the other end of the bar in a tent saloon. A canopy made from the same canvas had been staked out to keep the Mojave sun off the necks of the players and backstage personnel when they broke for lunch. They lined up along a trestle table crowded with covered pots heated by cans of Sterno: Indians in feathers who last week had been centurions in armor for DeMille, stunt gaffers with limps almost as bad as Randy's, women in homey bonnets, the same women next day in whores' silk, codgers with whiskers, tinhorns in tile hats, carpenters, painters, electricians, cowboys dressed as cowboys, and an undertaker in a morning coat who for some reason looked like Woodrow Wilson. They ate whatever the company brought from town, packed in ice in the original chuck wagon that appeared in the film and prepared by professional cooks.

The third day on location, Frank held out his bowl and stared at the man in the apron ladling clam chowder into it from the other side of the table.

"Long time no see, Frank," said Randy. "You want crackers?"

THIRTY-ONE

In some languages there is no word for good-bye. One cannot help but think it was a conscious decision, and reflect upon its wisdom.

"Well, I sure don't want no biscuits. There's a cowboy working for Famous Players still digesting it from Colorado."

Randy turned to his assistant, a tall bony kid with pimples like smallpox pustules. "Finish this out, will you? I'd go easy on the chili. I didn't put in no green ones, but it's commencing to look like a Christmas wreath. No sense poisoning no stars."

He helped himself to a bowl of chowder and a cube of cornbread that looked like rotten concrete and accompanied Frank to another trestle table, away from a group of wranglers sweetening their coffee from a bottle. Frank asked if they should borrow it.

"Go ahead if you want. I give up that hoo-head john after Nome."

"I don't much need it. Once you drank otter piss in an

Aleut camp it ruins you for everything else." They were sitting across from each other. Frank blew steam off a spoonful from his bowl. "What you been up to, Randy?"

"This and that. You?"

"Same thing, I reckon. You still lugging that smokewagon?"

"Been wearing it so long I took it into the shower last week. Still got that Remington?"

"It's my good luck piece, saved me from the rope in Fort Smith. What become of that Ballard rifle?"

"Sold it for grub. What become of that Winchester?"

"The same. Country's got so crowded you don't need no long gun to drop a man."

"Yakima Jim died last week of pure mean and blood poisoning over a poker game; little bitty belly gun fired so close it set his shirt afire. World's shrunk and no mistake."

"You still unattached?"

"I taken up with a woman in Glenwood Springs. We never said the vows, but she used my name and had a kid she said was mine, but I got my doubts."

"I hope you're right. I wouldn't want to think there's another Locke running around pretending to be a human being. She leave you?"

"Sure did. The doc said it was dropsy, but she told me near the end it was a broken heart and I was the reason. I was always running off, leaving her alone to chase down some rumor of you."

"I believe that."

"Maybe so, but if her heart was broke it sure didn't affect her appetite. By the time she took sick I bet she bent the scale at two hunnert. Galloping her was like trying to hang onto a sack of beans in a runaway wagon. What about you? Ever marry?"

"Yes, sir. Still am."

"Hell you say."

"Even so. We sleep in what you might call separate bedrooms. Hers is in Boston, Massachusetts."

"Same issue?"

"There was several, but I calculate that one topped the list." Frank swallowed a hunk of clam; it went down without chewing. "Ever hear from Cripplehorn?"

"I heard he tried to get into pictures, then went back East and died."

"I heard the same, though it was a tame fit of apoplexy. He's laying in a Sisters of Charity home in Atlantic City, New Jersey, drinking his supper through a straw."

"I don't envy them sisters. I don't know how you put up with him in that shack in Frisco."

"He was a big sissy. I took the borrow of his toothbrush once and never heard the end of it. He was always saying how when he got rich he was going to trade that ivory eye for a glass one made in Vienna, hire some fellow named Mo-nay to paint it."

"I'm surprised you didn't shoot him."

"I considered it, but he talked so pretty I figured I'd miss him. It was like listening to Scripture."

"He was a tinhorn through-and-through. I don't believe he ever read a book, much less wrote one. He got himself into some silk-hat company somehow and remembered everything he heard."

"He weren't stupid. Them vendors in that tent in the Strip kicked back half of every pail of beer they sold. He kept the tally in a bitty notebook."

"I'd bet a good saddle he never showed it to that Sheridan Weber."

The assistant director, a consumptive-looking New Englander with a ladylike strut, blew his whistle. They had five minutes before the next take.

Randy said, "I'm going to shoot him next."

"He's just doing his job."

"I'm going to shove that whistle down his gullet first."

Frank changed the subject. "You know, we just missed each other in Carson City last year. I checked in to the Empress Catherine just after you checked out."

"I caught the last train to Gunnison. Sewing-machine drummer I run into in the vertical railway said he talked to a fellow named Farmer there last week. Said he packed a forty-five Remington."

"You should stay off elevators. One day that door may slide open and there I'll be."

"I thought the whole point of this confab was to put that to rest."

Frank paused with his spoon halfway to his mouth. "You talking truce?"

"No, sir, I don't speak that lingo."

They slurped soup in silence for a minute.

Frank said, "I don't like leaving no job half-finished. That director fellow says we wrap next week. He's hosting a party at the Watering Hole."

"I reckon I'll see you there." Randy stood and picked up his bowl. "Whatever happened to that Dutch ear, by the way?"

The place was got up like every saloon in the West, or what some easterner thought it would look like. A fat naked woman lollopped in a chaise longue in a scrolled frame above the backbar, drilled through with authentic-looking bullet holes, and an eight-gauge shotgun was growing dust on a rack made of elk antlers above a Faro table where a group of extras sat drinking and not gambling. The string band that had played throughout the production to create a proper mood played a piece composed for the piano players who would accompany the showings. The director made a speech, said nobody's money was good in the joint beyond the first two drinks, and sat down at a table with the female lead and the brave lieutenant who'd led the suicide charge against about ten thousand Apaches, a young Shakespearean actor from Hartford, Connecticut. The female lead didn't appear to object when the director put an arm around her and squeezed a breast.

Randy had come there straight from the set, where the

assistant director was shooting second-unit to fill out the rest of the reel, and cast him as a stove-up stagecoach driver. He wore the costume he'd been given from the wardrobe grab-bag—sweat-stained Stetson with the brim turned up in front, shirt made of ticking, patched dungarees tucked into stovepipe boots with the heels ground down by dozens of pairs of feet. He spotted a pair of slumped shoulders he knew as well as his own at the end of the packed bar. He left the fake Indian he'd been talking with in the middle of a drunken gripe and went over to tap one of those shoulders. He wore his Colt in a prop holster, his old one having worn out in the Oklahoma oil fields. The new one was stiff enough to hold a flagpole; the pistol slid out every time he'd mounted to the driver's seat.

No tap was needed. Frank sensed his presence and turned quickly from the bar, resting his hand on his Remington. He had on a regular suit of clothes and a pearl-gray bowler he'd swiped from Wardrobe, also a stiff slick holster just like Randy's, with a tie-down that made a two-handed draw unnecessary and a hammer thong to keep the pistol where it belonged.

"How do, Frank?" Randy spoke as if they hadn't seen each other only last week.

"Not so bad, Randy. Yourself?"

"Middling."

"I forgot to ask you how you found L.A."

"I got off the train and there it was."

The conversation lapsed. Both men looked embarrassed

after this exchange. They'd talked themselves out in the tent commissary. After so much time they had only the one thing in common.

"Where you want to do this?" Randy asked.

"It's still light out."

They went outside, Randy first on account of his leg. He'd sooner expect a priest of the faith to backshoot him than Frank.

It was suppertime. Traffic was light. They waited for a streetcar to pass, then stepped out onto the asphalt and faced off.

There was no need for talk or signals, no whenever-you're-readies or dropping of bandannas: That was for Jack Dodger books and moving pictures. When each man was satisfied the other was set, they went for their pistols.

Both men were at a disadvantage. They were unfamiliar with the fast draw, which hadn't existed before eastern fabulists invented it, and slower than any movie pistoleer; but Randy had an edge. Frank forgot about the hammer thong, and fumbled with it when the Remington didn't clear. Randy's slug pierced his heart just as he got the rig loose. Frank fell cruciform on his back in the middle of Cahuenga Boulevard and didn't twitch.

Randy didn't bother to check for signs of life; he'd known the outcome the moment the pistol pulsed in his hand. He dropped it back into its holster and turned away.

A crowd gathered around the dead man, some of them cowboys from the Watering Hole drawn by the familiar sound of gunfire. The director and his two leads hung back in the doorway. A police officer in harness came blasting his whistle to clear a path. No one paid any attention to the elderly bean-slinger hobbling in the opposite direction.

On the sidewalk, Randy whistled an old cattle lullaby, waiting for the next streetcar to come racing along. When it did, he stepped out in front of it.